# SINS OF THE DAUGHTER

FRANK LUCIANUS

ISBN: 978-1-925988-34-5

# CONTENTS

# PROLOGUE

## CORNERSTONE

The room was dark. Only but the tip of the cigarette was visible into the darkness, shining like a small star in a night sky filled with clouds. A drag from the cigarette created a small faint light into the room, followed by a thick cloud of smoke, like the chimney of a factory, producing goods at a slow rate.

Jessica plucked the cigarette's ashes into the ashtray and took another drag, closing her eyes shut, as if the light from the tip blinded her. She was lost in her thoughts, trying to solve everything at once. She saw him looking at her. His eyes. His warm smile. Francesco's form wouldn't leave. It was as if he never died. He never left. It was as if he was always there, by her side, supporting, in her every decision.

The ashtray had already seventeen cigarettes in it and Jessica put out another, moving it in a circular motion inside the ashtray as though she was searching for something underneath the ashes. She turned on the desk lamp, shedding a faint light inside the office, revealing the thick veil of smoke floating into the air. Her father's old office was now covered in fumes. He would have scolded her for smoking in there, but he was no longer around.

The mess on her desk would surprise anyone, but not Jessica. She had so many things in her head and had to deal with all at once. The only thing standing out was a letter; a yellowish paper stained with letters from a typewriter. She grabbed the letter and read it.

*Dear sister,*

*I was glad when I learned you came back from Italy. I'm sorry I couldn't be there to greet you properly but people aren't allowed to have visitors or take trips into the city.*

*I'm sorry I couldn't be there for the birth of my nephew and your wedding. I hope Alberto's treating you well. I know it was hard for you to move on, but I hope it's for the best.*

*Kiss my nephew for me. I hope you're back for a good reason. Don't do anything stupid.*

With love
-Giovanni

Tears overwhelmed her eyes, forming a small river down her cheeks. A drop of tears found its way to her chin and dropped on the paper. Her hand was trembling as she put it down. She grabbed another cigarette from her package. Another cloud of smoke flew into the air.

Jessica closed her eyes shut and leaned back in her chair. Another tear moved down towards her chin but she wiped it with the back of her hand before it reached her black dress. She was lost once again into her own thoughts.

A soft tap on the door pulled her out of her dreams as if she resurfaced out of the sea after a long dive under the water. She opened her wet red eyes wide open. "Come in." She said clearing her throat.

Sofia opened the door. "Are you busy?" she asked with a soft voice still standing at the doorstep. "No mother. Please come in." Jessica said with a crack in her voice, struggling to hide her emotions. "I took Luca back to his bed. He fell asleep on the couch" she said with a warm smile. The same warm smile she always had while talking about her grandson. "How are you?" Sofia took a seat across Jessica, letting the light wash over her face.

Jessica took a drag from the cigarette. Sofia looked more tired than ever. Her face looked broken, filled with wrinkles as if she grew older overnight. She was still a beautiful woman, with her silver lines in her hair giving her a charming aura. Nevertheless, most of the time she looked more weakened than charming. "I'm fine" Jessica muttered after a long pause and took another drag, trying to seem unconcerned of her troubles.

"Reading Giovanni's letter again?" Sofia shined a

sympathetic smile to Jessica. "It's the only thing left of him."

"At least he's alive and well."

"Yes." was the only thing that came out of Jessica's mouth. She was not sure how to feel about her family situation. There were times she thought that Francesco and her grandmother were the lucky ones. They were those who managed to be relieved of the family's burden and moved on to a better place. Jessica made the sign of the cross and took another drag.

Sofia followed Jessica's example. "It's not easy moving on," she said as her warm smile vanished. The same tired look painted her face. A look that was dark and exhausted.

"It's not Sofia. I'm not sure I could if it wasn't for Luca…or you."

"You are my life now Jessica. I'll stand by your side. At least, you have Alberto now."

Jessica scoffed to the sound of Alberto's name. "Yeah. Lucky me," she said with an ironic tone. "I know it wasn't a marriage based on love…"

"It definitely wasn't."

"But he loves you, Jessica."

"I guess. My only concern is Luca and the family."

The pressure got heavier in the room as silence sat down to the thick smoke of Jessica's cigarettes. The two women were sitting still, each one lost in their own thoughts, looking in the darkest corners of the room.

"So. Now that we are back. What's the plan?"

"I don't know. I'm lost. My father had the details of all the families in New York. Information, names..." Jessica paused to take another drag as if she was searching for the right words to say. "But things have changed."

"Changed how?"

"Word in the street is that the Jews control the booze business. Jamaicans are smuggling guns and trafficking and our beloved Chinese control the drug market."

"Different times indeed. We live on for a few years and New York has turned into a buco di culo." Sofia said with frustration in her voice. Her expression betrayed that she looked back to the good old days when Luca used to have the entire city under his thumb. Even when Michael came, trying to take over the city from Luca, they were both capable leaders, keeping the streets clean.

"I came back to clean this buco di culo, Sofia. Vacation time is over." Jessica said with determination in her voice, putting out the cigarette, reaching for another.

"Jessica..." Sofia said and paused, trying to find the best words to describe her concerns without attacking or insulting her.

"We discussed this. This is a dangerous game."

"Save it, Sofia. I respect you and your judgment. But there's nothing to discuss."

"Think of your son, Jessica. Do you want him to end up like us? Alone?"

"I don't want him to end up like me. Hating the cops for taking away his father. Hating the Saltinottis for taking away his uncles." Jessica hissed as her eyes cramped as she lit up another cigarette.

Sofia took a short breath. She knew Jessica had every right in the world to feel that way. She still felt that way. Both of her sons' deaths to the hands of organized crime. However, Sofia made her peace with it. Something that Jessica couldn't do. Sofia crossed her arms on the desk.

"If I can't change your mind, at least let me help you." Sofia tried to hide the uneasiness in her voice. Jessica kept staring at her, waiting for her proposition.

"I've been in this business longer than you."

"Sofia, I don't want another lecture."

"I'm not going to give you one. I want to help you find peace."

"So, what do we do?" Jessica asked, almost ignoring Sofia's concerns.

"We are short in numbers. We need New York's Italian families to back us up."

"Do you have anyone in mind?"

"We can't count on the Saltinottis."

Jessica paused and her eyes almost spat fire. Her face took an outraged devilish look. "Don't mention that name again." she hissed and took a big drag from her cigarette.

"The Baldinottis are back in the game. We had our differences but they hate the…." Sofia paused trying to avoid saying the name, Saltinotti.

"They hate them as much as we do."

"Why is that?"

"Davide's daughter now run things and the Saltinottis are making her life a living hell."

"Davide's daughter?"

"Yes. Sabina. She struck a deal with Stefano and three days later, half of her assets were confiscated by the police."

"Why am I not surprised?"

"Apart from the Baldinottis, all the old loyal families to us would want to support us."

Jessica put out the cigarette and pressed her fist against her lips, thinking about the current situation. There were so many loose ends to take care of. Every time she felt under pressure, the image of Francesco and then her father would appear. She couldn't stop thinking about how did they stayed in control amidst the chaos.

"Have our men from Italy had a talk with them yet?"

"I think we should do it ourselves." Sofia disagreed and her tone turned serious. There were moments when the sadness faded and the powerful woman Sofia would take over. This was one of those moments. Jessica could see in her eyes that she already had a plan, at least something to start off.

"Seems like we are in driver's seat?"

"Exactly. We can't let them think we're hiding behind our men."

"I'll talk to Sabina then. It would be better if you keep your distance from her."

Sofia nodded pleased with Jessica's opinion. The assassination of Davide would make her as the mother of the assassin look very bad. They need Sabina on their side.

"What are we going to do with the gangs?"

"Once we have the families backing us, it's only a matter of time."

"I'm willing to go to war. As your husband and my father did."

"Jessica. Our men did a war for the wrong reasons. Many innocents died."

"I don't care. I don't care about the police or the other gangs. Our name and our sacrifices will not go in vain."

"Si ma… don't stray from our target as your father did."

"I know Sofia. I know."

Another moment of silence followed as both women stood there, drawn once again in their thoughts. Sofia kept staring at Jessica. Still determined to back her, but her eyes revealed a slight hint of dread. She didn't want to see her stepdaughter end up like the other members of her family.

Jessica's eyes narrowed, and she clenched her fist. Her nails were dipped inside of her palms, leaving three discrete marks. Her blood in her veins was boiling once again. Every time she thought about the Saltinottis or the police, images of her wedding kept coming back. She was frenzied. She had to take out all that frustration and anger and all those years she didn't have a single chance. Now, she had.

"Jessica. Keep your head in the game." Sofia pointed out sensing her impatience. "Your father…"

"I know!" Jessica lashed out at Sofia. "I know my father and your husband and my soon to be husband screwed everything up. I know!" she shouted. Sofia turned out to be her friend and the only person she could rely on after Alberto, but there were times Sofia's rational thinking and her constant lecturing drove her mad. Jessica knew the mistakes of both families, but she didn't want to sit idle until her mind became shrouded by hate. She needed to use that point of hate like a loaded gun towards the right target. It would be useless after she made amends with her situation. Nothing would drive her.

"I won't screw this up because I don't have the luxury to do so!" she kept shouting until she felt a sting in her throat. Jessica started coughing as if her lungs were begging for another drag. The coughing made her pause and made her eyes wet. She took a sip from her glass of whiskey that had been sitting on the desk for hours. The interruption made her relax.

Sofia kept looking on with tenderness in her eyes. She knew how Jessica felt. She had been there, but there was nothing she could say. She could only be there and make sure Jessica didn't do anything stupid.

The soft screeching on the door interrupted the heated conversation as the door opened. A young boy was standing at the doorstep with brown hair, dressed in silk pajamas, holding a light brown teddy bear in his hand. "Mammina? Are you okay?" the boy asked rubbing his eyes. Those eyes that reminded Jessica of Francesco. The boy had his eyes and she couldn't stop staring at them.

Jessica gasped and almost jumped out of her seat. "Si Luca. Si" she said with a warm tone. The same tone in her grandmother's voice. "Did Mamma wake you up?" Jessica said as she grabbed, giving him a long tight hug. "No. I couldn't sleep. Nonna didn't read me my favorite story." Luca said standing there still holding his teddy bear tight. "Let's read it together then, shall we?" Jessica said grabbing Luca by the hand. "Okay." the boy said and turned around.

Sofia kept looking at the two. Tears overcame her eyes. Jessica saw Francesco when she looked at the kid but Sofia kept seeing Manuel, her little boy. Jessica gave a warm look of relief at Sofia before leaving, heading to Luca's room. The only thing that brought her back to her senses was her lovely son. Her love for him was the same for his papa, Francesco.

1

—————

**DAVID ALLEN**

The 7th precinct was buzzing with constant chatter between its officers. They gathered in the main lobby, waiting for their captain to take the podium and give one of the most highly anticipated speeches of the year - an address about the current situation of organized crime in New York City.

The details weren't made available to the public and only a few knew of the exact details of the speech. New York City was being ran by new gangs of lawless bandits. The escalation in violence had reached an all-time high after the Bloodshed, a massacre that New York's crime families wanted to forget forever.

Despite the high number of police presence at the press conference, there were reporters from all of the local newspapers and television stations to report and broadcast the event live. There were some anxious media trying to get statements from the high-ranking officers present but the captain's orders were clear. *Do not talk to the press.*

More than half an hour had passed, and the media became more and more anxious. This could be the story that could launch their careers if today's announcement was attention-grabbing.

The captain of the 7th police precinct stepped slowly to the podium, a few feet away from the crowd. He looked tired and even at that moment, had the look of a person besieged by a thousands and one expectations.

He removed his hat and combed back his grey hair. Then he placed his arms behind his back, looking powerful. Despite his tired appearance, he appeared to be in control. Confident that everything would soon fall into place.

The lobby was lit up with a barrage of white camera flashes; everyone trying to capture the mood of the moment. The repeated flashes continued nonstop until the captain raised his palm. "Please," he said with a tone of authority. Most of the flashes had stopped like lamps reaching closer to their lifetime expectancy.

*"It's been almost five years since the Bloodshed headed by the law enforcement agencies of New York City in collaboration with the Federal Bureau of Investigation, ATF and other outside law enforcement agencies."*

Silence had overtaken the hall as he went on.

*"It's also been five years since the most notorious families in this city were put behind bars or taken out, thanks to the work of the good police officers that stand amongst us or have fallen."*

The captain cleared his throat and planned the next words that would come out of his mouth. He didn't read the notes he had prepared.

*"And still here we are. The violence of organized crime in New York is rising again. I've spent over twenty years in the force and it still saddens me to see good officers being lured into corruption, going against their vows to protect and serve."*

The captain's hand trembled, but he placed it behind his back to make it stop. It was a trembling resulting from his displeasure with the cloud of corruption that continues to linger despite all efforts to eradicate it. It also was a sign of fear knowing that there were those who wanted to take control of the city by unlawful means. The captain continued:

*"The Harpoons, the Triads, the Kosher Nostra, The Italians, The Albanian Boys. Just to name a few of those that come to mind when we talk about organized crime in our city. These bandits have decided they have the right to do as they please! We will rid our cities of these petty individuals. And yes, we have made big strides in weeding out corruption from our police force over the last few years, but there still lingers some of its remnants."*

The captain paused taking a sip of water close by, knowing that what he was going to say in the next few minutes would shake the room. Before then, he talked on ways that his police force was working to step up efforts to hire good officers and that there were still citizens who supported the police in their communities and they would continue to help reporting illegal activities. Then, the captain restated that a few bad cops have lead to internal chaos in the past and that we don't want to repeat these events.

*"I think it is time to address the issue of organized crime once and for all and give it the importance it deserves. We need someone to put an end to it in our city and bribery in our police ranks. Every police department in this city cannot do their jobs while the corrupt apples are spoiling the bunch. This is why…"*

The return of flashes and the sounds of cameras' clicking echoed the lobby, smothering the last words of the captain. The reporters were yelling in a loud buzzing with no meaning. The captain raised his hand but the noise only got louder.

His last statement left the media persons stunned. They were there to find the golden goose that would make them writer or reporter of the year. "Silence or I will have you removed," the captain yelled as the flashes stopped. The lobby returned to silence.

"This is why…" the captain repeated and took a few seconds to maintain his calmness.

*"We asked for the help of the Department of Justice once again and with the help of the CIA, FBI and ATF, they have given us a special task force to deal specifically with the organized crime criminals. This task force is named the OC Task Force."* With O.C. standing for Organized Crime.

Most that were present knew the captain and the mayor agreed to bring out the big guns for political reasons. Still, they stood there with their jaws dropped, unable to hide their emotions. The silence was drowned in sighs as everyone wanted for the captain to finish his address, so they can ask questions.

*"After many discussions with the mayor, we decided that it was time to let someone with no attachments to this city take over our law enforcement efforts, while we will stand by their side, providing all the support we can."*

The captain then turned to the side, looking deep at a small corner in the lobby. A tall man approached and took the captain's position on the podium.

The man was filled with confidence and had an aura of authority. His black hair, combed back with mousse, was bushy on both sides as it appeared that he was growing bald. Dressed in a black suit with a small pin of the American flag close to his neck, the man fixed his tie and cleared his throat.

"Thank you, captain, for filling in the people, but let me present my side of how our task force sees the situation" the man said with a deep voice. His voice was soothing but it could get harsh in the split of a second.

"My name is David Allen. I am the head of the new organized crime task force. I spent years working with the Bureau and the CIA. Your city is rotten to its core." he said and paused as the reporters started another stream of yells, this time along with some officers who were outraged by the statement.

David let the crowd go on, waiting like a teacher in a classroom for the children to stop. He knew he was in charge for now on. His patience and confident look made the shouts of the entire crowd fade away as if he had some kind of weird utopia.

*"The OC Task Force and I, along with the help of other law enforcement agencies will not tolerate any of this misconduct anymore. Your actions made Washington take a closer look and we cannot have New York bleeding again over a war headed by corruption with. From now, you all will report to me. I do not want any case going unreported. I will not tolerate any foolish requests for time offs and I will not tolerate any unprofessionalism. I was given the right to fire anyone who goes against my rules and God help me, I will abuse that power...."*

The man suddenly stopped and left the podium leaving everyone shocked.

The captain quickly came up again as everyone was frightened by the new crime fighting boss's introduction. "I will now answer any questions you may have." The captain knew that there would be a flood of shouting, camera flashes, and rebuttals that would be hurled his way.

Meanwhile, Special Agent, David Allen made his way back to his new office as the lobby was overwhelmed with noise like a concert of a pop star. He shut the door and still the noise found its way inside. Fixing his tie once again, he grabbed the phone and dialed the number of his commanding headquarters. "Sir. We are ready to begin the operation" he said in a tone of respect for hierarchy towards his superior.

"Excellent work, David. Keep me posted" the muffled old voice echoed on the other line.

"Yes, Commander." David hung up and took a seat behind his desk. He looked at his nearly-empty desk, returning a pen that was out of its position. *Perfect!* The files on all the organized crime gangs were on his left and police records on the right. The first file he picked up from the pile read *Giuliani*.

David began reading the file like a student preparing for the SATs, writing notes in his empty notebook in front of him. It was time to get rid of the hoodlums in this city, once and for all.

2

———

**THE FIRST PARTING**

Jessica was walking down downtown through the busy streets of New York City. The black scarf around her neck, was moving up and down on the top of her bosoms. Her eyes were concealed behind her sunglasses as the sunlight pierced the ground softly. Because of the cold, Jessica Lombardi could see her breath every second she exhaled.

Her son, Luca was walking beside her, wearing a green jacket and a black knitted cap. His cheeks were reddened and his green eyes stood out. He was holding his mother's hand tightly. His grip got tighter as they got closer to his new school. He was about to part from his mother for the first time.

His stomach tightened the moment they reached the front doors of the school. Luca looked upwards at his mother giving her worrisome look. Jessica smiled warmly; a smile that could melt away the cold. "We're here my baby" she said. Luca gasped as he couldn't find words to say. "Are you nervous?" Jessica asked playfully, teasing Luca.

"N-no." he stuttered.

"You shouldn't be. There's nothing to be afraid of."

"Will you be gone for a long time?" the boy asked embarrassed by his question.

"I'll be back in no time. Okay?"

"O-okay."

"If anything happens, I'll be here right away."

The boy smiled feeling safer, knowing his mother would be nearby.

"Make a few friends today, sweetheart. That is what school is for, my dear. Have some fun but listen to your teachers." Jessica winked. Luca trusted his mother and nodded.

"Did you like school when you were little?" the boy asked before going inside.

"I loved it! And I was pretty good at it." Jessica said playing with her hair. "You'll be good at it if you remember to have fun and do your work!" she pushed him softly in the back, to get his attention on the kids playing at the playground.

"Okay, mama."

Their conversation was interrupted when the principal of the school appeared at the front doors.

"Miss. Lombardi?"

"Giuliani." Jessica said in response.

"Principal Logan. Pleasure to meet you, Miss

Giulani." the principal took a step forward stretching out his hand. Jessica goes on and shakes it. "And you must be, Luca, my boy?" the principal said rubbing his head. "Let's go inside and see the other children. Shall we?" Taking the boy's hand, Luca nodded.

"Mr. Logan, don't let anything happen to my boy."

Principal Logan heard that over a million times and replied, "Don't worry, Miss. Guilani? Luca's in good hands."

Jessica stood there, watching the principal walk away with her little son. She felt a sharp pain inside her chest. Her breathing suddenly became heavier. She could feel the pain from her chest due to not being able to cope with leaving her son with strangers. Jessica wanted to have him around her at all times and couldn't take any chances of anything happening to him. Luca was the only male around in her household. He was only thing Francesco left her. It was the best parting gift that one could leave in his place.

Jessica smiled gingerly knowing that he would be okay. She put on her sunglasses and walked, heading to *the Baldinotti Residence, 72 Port Street, Fourth Floor, New York, New York.* It would take twenty minutes to reach, but she preferred to go alone without her bodyguards. She didn't want the unnecessary attention. No one knew she was back in town.

————

The streets of New York are always jam-packed. Jessica wasn't in a rush to reach Sabina's house, letting the memories of the past occupy her mind. The cold winter's air felt good giving her a feeling of euphoria. She detoured passing by Castello Di Vino, hoping to find Federico inside, but the ruined vacant sight made her feel sad.

The front entrance was boarded up, with shattered glass still lying on the pub's floor. There was yellow ribbon waving on the outside reading the words - *crime scene*. She peeped inside seeing the remains of bullet holes on the walls and around the counter. Everything was still intact but abandoned. There was an old sign in one of the windows reading *"For Sale"*.

Jessica took off her sunglasses, holding back her tears. She reflected on the special moments she had with Francesco inside that pub; the first drink, the day she first kissed him and the day they almost got killed. Then she remembered the biggest day of them all; the day they ran away and almost got married.

Then her mind shifted to Federico. He's probably spending his final days, broken just like his pub. But Jessica never forgot about him especially his cheerful mood even in the darkest of moments.

Jessica took a deep breath and hurried walking through the streets of New York. She vowed revenge for Francesco's death and owed her family a legacy. As she walked, her determination of upholding her end of the deal became set in stone.

**3**

---

## THE BOSS AWAKENS

Jacopo Saltinotti was sitting in the back of the "Palermo" restaurant, enjoying a glass of Franciacorta. The restaurant was empty, with only the owner and a waiter standing near the door, with the 'Closed' sign hanging in its front.

The tables were covered with argyle tablecloths, just like most Italian restaurants. Candles were placed in the middle of each table, next to small flowerpots, which made the place look expensive and hospitable. Only the candle on Jacopo's table was shedding its flickering light in the store, lighting up the dark corner of the restaurant. The blurred light entering the windows was not enough to brighten the whole place.

Jacopo grabbed a piece of Acceglio from the plate in front of him and finished his wine. He raised his arm, revealing his expensive golden watch, hiding under his expensive tailor-made Italian suit. He lifted his glass to the waiter to pour another glass of Franciacorta.

The waiter rushed to Jacopo's side, holding with respect an old dusty bottle. "Here you go, Don." The waiter then returned to his post as Jacopo nodded. He took another sip and gargled it as if he was a professional sommelier. He closed his eyes with joy as the exquisite taste trickled down his throat.

The sound of the bell rang as the door opened. A man dressed in a large black trench coat entered and hurried towards Jacopo's table. His curly black hair was messy and his receding hairline stood out. He was three times bigger than Jacopo. His fingers each had gold rings.

Despite his size, he was afraid of Jacopo. He reached the table and bowed, taking Jacopo's hand into his own and kissed it with respect. "Don Jacopo…" he said breathing heavily, taking a seat on the other side of the table.

Without saying a word, Jacopo took out a small wooden comb out of his pocket and combed his black hair to the side. "When did I give you permission to sit?" Jacopo found the fat man's conduct hilarious. The man's face was painted with panic as he struggled to stand up. "You are interrupting my wine hour"

"I- I know." the fat man stuttered taking a step away from the table.

"What's so important to disturb my tea time?"

"Don Jacopo." the man's voice trembled as Jacopo

lifted his glass and took another sip. His dark blue eyes staring deep inside the fat man's.

"I'm listening." Jacopo signaled the man to continue.

"There are some rumors in the street, Don. It is said that Jessica Lombardi's back in town." the fat man said avoiding Jacopo's sight.

Before Jacopo took another sip, he froze. Then he put the glass on the table slowly as if time was in slow motion. "What the fuck?"

"Jessica Lom-"

"I heard you the first time. When did you hear this?"

"Yesterday afternoon, Boss. One of my men said he saw her and her family at the port." the fat man started taking a step back from the table. Jacopo smiled but his face revealed something bad was about to happen. It was a smile that made the waiter take a few steps closer to the back of the restaurant.

"So, I presume that your men didn't see her today, right?" Jacopo hobbled like a man who had trouble standing up.

"N-no, Boss. It was only yesterday." the fat man took another step backward, plunging into a stool, making it fall to the ground.

"And did we follow her?" Jacopo started walking towards the man.

"I was only informed by my men yesterday. Please, I can ex-" the fat man's sentence was interrupted by Jacopo's fist landing on his face. Then landing on his ear, making him lose his balance.

The man's head was ringing as if a grenade exploded inside the restaurant. He raised his arms, almost as if he was pleading for his life. Another fist landed on his nose. The fat man felt his nose crack. His eyes were filled with tears. He wanted to scream, but he couldn't in front of the Don.

Jacopo cracked his knuckles as the fat man was moving further backwards in a state of drunkenness and desperation. "You didn't think to tell me yesterday afternoon?" Jacopo punched the man again in the face and then on his right temple, sending the man down on the floor. The man raised his arms to cover his face but Jacopo was landing punch after punch.

"I came here as soon…" the man tried to say but another punch interrupted him. Blood sprayed out of his mouth and his lips and face were swollen.

Jacopo sat on the man's big belly and kept punching him in the face. The man tried defending himself but Jacopo had struck him too many times. His reflexes weren't quick enough and Jacopo had him pinned down on the ground. Jacopo kept punching until the man stopped moving completely.

The waiter and the owner of the restaurant were hiding speechless. The waiter was almost near the exit while the owner was peeking from behind the counter. Jacopo got up taking off his white suit, covered in blood, like an artist who created a modern piece of art. His suit fall off his shoulders, revealing his black vest and silver Smith and Wesson dangling on his waist. He went back to his seat and took another of the Franciacorta while cleaning the blood from his hands with a velvet towel.

"Clean this mess up now and get me a phone."

"Yes, Don," the owner responded.

Jacopo sat thinking deeply, acting as if nothing had happened. The fat man with the gold rings was dead on the floor and Jacopo didn't give a fuck.

## 4

## 72 PORT STREET, NEW YORK, NY

Jessica was standing outside an old rusted building with cracks on its walls, ready to collapse. The smell of the docks brought back memories of her first assignment by a father to try to entice Elias. This time it would be much different.

The number 72 was written on an old bronze sign. The lot appeared vacant as if no one was living inside. Jessica walked through the small-withered garden in the front, reaching the main entrance. She looked at the names on the apartment phones - Sabina Baldinotti, Apartment 4C. That's hers.

She entered inside heading towards an old elevator shaft and pressed button four. The elevator rumbled; a sign it need to be replaced soon.

The fourth floor was filled with the smell of chicken soup. Jessica walked on its purple carpet searching for apartment 4C. Once she reached the end of the corridor, she spotted the door. She recalled her first mission with her brother, Giovanni as she knocked on the door.

A few moments later, heavy footsteps could be heard behind the door. "Who is it?" a deep voice asked.

"Jessica Lombardi." Hearing that name, the door suddenly unlocked. There a big man looked at her through the crack, with the latch hanging on the door.

"Who are you again?" the man asked scratching his beard.

"I'm the head of the Lombardi family." Jessica responded unfazed by the man's intimidating voice.

"Wait here." the man closed the door and returned a few moments later. The door was opened, with the man blocking the entrance. "Any weapons?" he asked taking a step closer. Jessica lifted her purse and handing it to the man.

"Here you go."

The man opened the purse and turned it upside down, dropping its contents on the ground. Makeup, tissues and a car key fell out.

"I have no metal on me."

The big man then told Jessica that he had orders to pat her down.

"Go ahead."

He patted her legs up to her thighs. Jessica knew he was a pervert by the way he slowly moved upwards. If she contested, then her meeting would be in jeopardy.

Afterwards, the man threw the bag back at her and moved to the side. "Sabina is waiting for you." he said extending his arm, urging Jessica to come inside. Jessica picked up her things from the ground and walked inside with the poise of a woman who owned the building.

The apartment was nothing like the outside of the building. The interior was covered with a silky gray carpet. The kitchen was decorated and every surface seemed to reflect like a mirror. Sabina was sitting in the living room, drinking a cup of tea, which made the whole room smell like exotic fruits.

Jessica entered and saw Sabina for the first time in years. She was a young girl in her twenties dressed in tight workout gear. Sabina smiled and nodded for Jessica to sit down. Jessica leaned over to kiss her hand.

As Jessica did so, the man yelled from the back. "Keep your distance from the Donna!"

"It's okay, Carl." Jessica took a seat on the sofa across from Sabina.

"Pleasure to see you, Sabina. It's been years." Jessica took off her sunglasses placing them inside her purse.

"The notorious - Jessica Lombardi. Would you like a cup of tea?"

"Yes, please." Jessica said trying not to insult her.

"You heard the Donna, Carl. Hurry." the man went to the kitchen.

"How was your trip?" Sabina asked proud about Jessica's return to New York.

"I'm still getting used to it." Jessica didn't want to feel intimidated by the young girl in front of her.

"How's the things in New York?"

"I think you already know."

"I do know and just wanted to know your thoughts on how things are on the frontline, Donna."

"You try to do something good for the Italians and you get screwed over."

"So, I heard."

A moment of awkward silence followed with only the kettle on the fire whistling like a train ready to leave. Sabina stared at Jessica as if she was trying to learn everything she could. Sabina's bodyguard entered the living room, handing Jessica a cup.

"Leave us to be, Carl." the man left the room closing the doors. Jessica took a sip and put the mug on the table in front of her.

"So. To what do I owe the pleasure?" Sabina opened smiling. Jessica smiled back, glad that Sabina to started off. It was a trick Sofia told her from the old ways of the Italians to gain leverage in any discussion.

"We have a lot to discuss."

"I expected you much sooner, Donna Jessica."

"You did?"

"The only Lombardi alive, or out of prison returns to New York. There must be a good explanation for your coming."

"There is actually."

"Shall I feel honored?"

"Feel honored for what?"

"Aren't you here to ask for my help?"

Jessica chuckled. This girl is too confident and haven't

proved her worth yet. It's obvious that the Baldinottis haven't taught her manners either.

"I am actually, yes."

"Then, I'm listening." Sabina said crossing her legs.

"I heard you were screwed over by the Saltinottis and…"

"And you want my help to take them down."

"Since you already know so much, why don't you tell me your terms, Sabina?"

"Fifty percent of the business" she said playfully but serious.

"What business?"

"The one we will run."

"Don't you think your number is over the top for what you can offer, Sabina?"

"Is it?"

Jessica was feeling bullied by this youngster. However, the Baldinotti girl had some wit that Jessica was beginning to like. Jessica took a deep breath, trying to regain control of the conversation.

"Yes, it is Sabina. You need me as much as I need you? Don't you?"

"And why is that?" she said leaning closer.

"The Saltinottis almost took away everything you own. Do you think you can survive alone?"

"The Saltinottis are not my concern right now, Donna Jessica."

"Let's cut the crap, Sabina. With the Jamaicans

controlling the guns, you have no business to run in this city."

Sabina leaned back and Jessica knew she had just hit her nerve. All she had to do was keep pushing. "I know you struck a deal with the Saltinottis to get back into the gun business while I was gone and they didn't meet their end of the bargain."

"What if I told you I could get you control off the gun market once again and make you Donna over the Saltinottis?"

"I can't go against them. Not after what they've done."

"You'd be crazy to do business with them alone. I'm offering an alliance."

"The Baldinottis with the Lombardis?"

"And the Giulianis!"

Sabina's face was full of disgust. That name *"Guilani"* was the nail in the coffin. Francesco killed her father. "That is why I want fifty percent of the business." she spat warning Jessica. "Do you think I will work with the fottuto family that killed my father? Do you want me to say thank you as well, *brutto figlio di puttana*?" Sabina kept ranting.

Jessica listened waiting calmly for her to end.

"Yes and I apologize." Sabina surprised by Jessica's statement, smiled arrogantly.

"Your father tried to go behind the Giulianis backs."

"He went behind their backs to help you, Lombardis!"

"You know the rules, Sabina. It was a tragedy but…"

"How dare you?"

"If the Giulianis are evil, then the Saltinottis are the devils, Sabina." Jessica shouted and the bodyguard in the next room ran into the living room. Sabina gestured for him that everything was okay. "What do you want from me, Jessica Lombardi?"

"An alliance. The gun market is yours and I want fifteen percent. This is my final offer. You can either join me or stay here and watch your father's empire collapse."

"I won't tolerate the Giulianis messing around in my business."

"They won't. They have the upmost respect for you and will honor my wishes in regards to you."

"And Sofia? I heard she came back with you. I believe you already started an alliance."

"We are one family. There is no alliance yet. I will be organizing the families to form one."

Sabina stood up pondering over Jessica's proposition.

"I won't let my pride ruin my family's business." she said smiling at Jessica; the same playful smile she had at the beginning. "When do we meet, Donna Jessica?" she said with a tone of respect.

"I will be calling a meeting for the Italian families to come, inviting them to join as one family. We will take over every single gang's business in New York including the Salinottis. New York belongs to us and us alone." Jessica said clenching her fists.

"It's a pleasure to do business with you." Sabina said

standing up, crouching over to kiss Jessica's hand. Jessica pulled it back quickly as if Sabina displeased her.

"No need for formalities, Sabina. I want to know I can trust you with my life."

"You can." Sabina said holding Jessica's hand.

"I got to get going. You'll be updated about the meeting." Jessica said in a hurry, leaving Sabina and the big man inside the living room.

Jessica exited the building, happy that she struck her first deal on her own. Her plan to bring together the families was a step closer in becoming reality.

## 5

# A FRIEND FROM THE PAST

Sofia was sitting on a cold bench across the street from Luca's school. She spent the last thirty minutes waiting for the school to dismiss the children for the day. The cold winds passed through her hair, making them wave like a flag. Sofia kept looking left and right expecting the unexpected; the instincts of a Don's widow.

A man in a black suit, wearing sunglasses walked towards her and took a seat. "Glad you are back." the man said looking straight ahead at the school, as if he was waiting for his child to walk outside the schoolyard.

"I'm glad, I'm back. Too much damn pasta and good wine" Sofia said laughing faintly which looking at grandson's school.

"What was that phone call about?"

"We're back in business."

"We?"

"Jessica Lombardi and I."

"Michael's bambina?"

"Si."

"How? Why?"

"You know why, Andrea."

The man nodded while Sofia wasn't looking at him. "Since…" the man paused.

"Since my husband's death, we've been hunted like rabid animals. That's why we're back to take control of New York once again."

"That Stronzo Jacopo. He's the worst thing that could ever happened to the us, Italians here in New York."

"Who?"

"Jacopo Saltinotti. The *merda's* a psychopath."

"He's running things down here now? I thought he was just a Soldato."

"He was."

"But?"

"But desperate times require desperate measures."

Sofia felt sad as if she was the one to blame for this madness.

"So, how can I help?"

"We're forming an alliance with the families."

"Impossible."

"Jessica had already talked to Sabina."

"She'll never side with you after what your son had done."

"She already has agreed to. It's not about one family being in control."

"Then what?" the man asked and stopped realizing that he answered his own question. The man nodded realizing what Sofia meant.

"Anyone else?"

"No. You're the first I've reached out to personally."

"I'm glad you did. You know I was always loyal to Luca."

"I know I can trust you, my good friend."

"You can. We've been out of the game a long time."

"So have we, Andrea."

Both remained silent for a moment. Andrea's face had lit up like a lighthouse seen in the distance of a dark sea. He thought about the good old days when Sofia and Luca were on top and how his empire flourished.

"Okay, I'm in."

"I knew you would be. Anyone else I need to reach out to?"

"We're like livestock with no farmers. Reach out to the Episcopos and Fondas." The man lowered his voice wanted to keep this between him and Sofia.

"The Episcopos are still in the business of building churches?"

"That's the only thing they have now. They'll want to join."

"Thank you, Andrea. We'll be having a family dinner in three days. I expect you to be there."

"It's great to see you back, Sofia."

"Likewise."

"New York needs you now more than ever." Andrea got up, holding his hat, so it wouldn't be blown away and walked down the road as if he was never there.

Sofia remained there proudly smiling. She was respected and most feared by the old Dons of New York City. Luca's name still had prominence. The new gangsters in town will soon realize. Her eyes shedded tears thinks about the old days of Michael and Luca. The mutual respect they had for each other's territories. Nowadays, no one respects no one even amongst the Italians.

A few minutes later, the school bell rang, and the schoolyard was filled with kids, running around in paradise. A flood of little kids stood on the pavement outside the school and among them, Sofia's grandson, Luca smiling. Sofia walked over, rubbing his head and grabbing him by the hand. The two of them walked home, going over Luca's first day at school. He was excited to meet new friends.

## 6

## HOSPITAL VISIT

Jessica passed through the walls of the hospital noticing dozens of patients in the lobbies waiting for their test results to come back and demanding that the doctors hurry up and see them.

Her heart pounded heavily with each step she took closer to Room 2A. The room where her father was resided in for the last five years.

Jessica reached the outside of her father's room, her hand was about to brace the silver door handle when she paused. She felt like a contestant who was about to open a mystery door. Once she went inside, she took a seat on an old green armchair.

The sound of the heart rate monitor was in sync with the voice of a reporter on TV. Then, the top of the news-hour main headline popped up on the screen: *Organized crime is coming to an end in New York.* This headline has been in all the daily papers and news outlets for the past few days. Jessica grabbed the remote control and shut off the TV, focusing on the rhythmical beeping of her father's heart monitor.

Michael was lying lifeless on the bed with two plastic tubes inside his nostrils. His eyes were closed shut and he seemed to be in a state of peace. He looked at least forty pounds thinner than the last time Jessica saw him. He was like a skeleton being kept alive.

There were no signs of injuries. It's been five years since the Bloodshed and still he hasn't recovered. Giovanni did his best to take care of father but now he's in jail, no one was around to check on the Don. Luca's old body just seemed as if it was just passing time with no value. Jessica placed her sunglasses on the bed stand and grabbed her father's hand. She squeezed his like a young girl when she's afraid, hoping to get some comfort from her parents. It felt like the same squeeze, young Luca gave her earlier in the day on the way to school.

"Hey, Papa." Jessica muttered as she held back the tears trying to crawl down her cheeks. "I miss you so much." she said noticing the serum tube that pierced his palm. "I'm back for you." Jessica was unable to find the right words. She watched him closely, thinking of all the moments they spent together.

"We never got the chance to talk after what happened," Jessica continued. "I've missed you so much." The tears on her cheeks were running loose, but she didn't care. She didn't even try to hold back now.

"Giovanni's in prison. He's having a hard time, but still alive. For now at least," Jessica paused grabbing a paper towel and blowing her nose. "I'm back to run our family business, Papa."

"Remember when you told me I'm not cut out for this? Remember when I screwed up over and over again?" she pretended to wait for his answer. "I struck a deal with Sabina. A bad deal if you ask me. But it's a deal, right?" Jessica was desperate for her father's approval. She wanted to hear his voice, telling her how much he loved her. How proud he was and how they would run the business together. How he would help her take revenge for Serena, for Francesco.

"How did you do it? How did you set aside your differences aside and work with Luca? How were you not blinded by hatred?" she kept asking pressing her father's hand against her forehead. "I want to do this right. I can't stop thinking about you and Francesco. I want to run the business right, like you both did..." Jessica paused.

Her emotions of vengeance began to form. She was talking to herself although her father was there. He was in a deep coma. "I want them these Salinottis to suffer like we did. I want them to die, knowing I was the reason for their deaths. Our dynasty must remain alive!" Jessica raised her voice without realizing she was almost shouting. " I want..." she broke down once again.

"I want you to come back, Papa. I need you now more than ever. You, Serena and Francesco. I need you all here. You knew about all this family business stuff. I'm not like you. I'm not…" Jessica hid her face, crying on the bedsheets; crying like the day she lost them and almost everything.

Jessica rose up and wiped the tears off of her face. She took a long deep breath, regaining control over her wild sentiments. She was like a rider taming a wild horse. "I married when I went back to Italy, Papa." Jessica laughed awkwardly. "I know it's weird and don't know if it was love, or my way to move on. Alberto's a nice guy. and loves me. I can never love or trust him like Francesco."

"It was nice talking to you. It's been so long" Jessica said putting on her sunglasses. "I love you, Papa." Jessica kissed him on the forehead and exited out of the room, walking by the patients still waiting and suffering just like Jessica and her father.

## 7

## ZHANG WEI'S OFFICE

Mr. Zhang Wei was sitting in a meeting room inside one of his factories. The windows were broken, letting a soft gust of wind inside. The temperature was colder than usual and the table was big enough to host more than ten. But only Zhang was there alone with a porcelain teapot in front of him. Two porcelain mugs with pink flowers were the only decoration son display.

The smell of Dragon Pearl Jasmine was stuffing his nostrils, blocking out all the odors outside. Three armed men were standing by the doors, holding Uzis. Silence overtook the place unless ordered otherwise. Zhang took a sniff from the teapot and the pot's steam made his glasses blurry. He put his glasses down and cleaned them with a black silky handkerchief with a golden crest swords printed on it.

A few minutes passed by when the doors opened

causing a grinding sound like metal hitting the ground. Zhang turned around calmly under the flickering lamps that made the place look like an old abandoned hospital. The guards held their guns tightly. Footsteps could be heard afar, and a man dressed in a white suit suddenly emerged through the gloom.

"Jacopo!" Zhang stood up offering a bow of respect. Jacopo walked fast ignoring him and grabbed a seat.

"Mr. Zhang." he said calmly.

"All alone?" the man asked in broken English.

"Si," answered Jacopo crossing his hands on the table.

"Good." Zhang said taking a seat, annoyed by Jacopo's behavior.

"My time is precious, Mr. Zhang. I suggest we get to the matter right away." Jacopo said looking at his nails, making sure they were perfect.

"Let's have tea first" Zhang proposed raising the teapot towards Jacopo.

"No time for drinks." Jacopo said leaning back in his chair.

"Okay. We, Triads, need your help, Mr. Jacopo." Zhang poured tea inside his mug.

"And why is that?"

"The new Task Force. They're going to be up our asses for awhile." Zhang blew, cooling off his tea.

"And how can my business help?"

"We need to use your routes to smuggle our priceless goods from China."

"Haha. Priceless? That's funny. Okay, but what do I get in return?"

"A nice part of my business?" Zhang said feeling his proposition was fair.

"Twenty percent."

"That's crazy." Zhang almost choked on his tea.

"Five percent."

"Twenty fucking percent."

"This is no way to negotiate Jacopo. Ten percent and that is my last offer."

"Look, Zhang. You need us and we don't need you. Am I correct?"

Zhang scratched his bald head. "You're not the only one with routes."

"We will be in a matter of months and you know this. Fifteen percent and when the time comes, you'll side with me. This is my final offer."

"When will be this time?"

"You will know. Do we have a deal, Mr. Zhang?" Jacopo gave his hand to Zhang.

"I guess we do."

Jacopo stood up like something was biting him in the chair and rushed out. "Starting tomorrow, our men will be by to give you the layouts." Jacopo's voice echoed the warehouse as he disappeared in its darkness.

## 8

## FINDING ALLIES

Jessica returned home for a few hours, sitting behind her father's desk, going over his notes. It was something she had been doing for the past few days, often spending hours looking at the history of the crime families of New York City. She needed to know everything she could on her father's dealings. Her father, Michael Lombardi was an expert and unfortunately, he wasn't around for Jessica to answer her questions.

Giovanni's letter was still lying on the messy desk. She read her brother's letter a few times which gave her a weird sense of purpose. Jessica noted details about Sabina Baldinotti's operation.

The soft knock on the door never reached Jessica's ears. Another one and a man came inside, making very little noise. Jessica still hadn't realized he walked in, taking a seat on the couch across the room. Jessica was snapped out of her thoughts when the man cleared his throat.

"Alberto, tesoro mio!" Jessica gasped rattled.

"I'm sorry. I didn't mean to scare you." he said scratching his shaven face.

Jessica looked at his honey brown eyes. She swore that those eyes could make her melt away.

"Working again?"

"As usual."

Alberto stood up and walked behind her, placing his hands on her shoulders. Massaging her, he said, "You feel tense" in a low sexy voice. "Should I help you rest?"

"Not right now, tesoro mio." Jessica said pulling away. Alberto looked confused and went back to the couch. "I feel like you've been avoiding me since the day we got back from Italy." He sounded like a child not getting enough attention.

"I know. But…"

"I get it. We've talked about this moment a thousand times."

"Grazie per la pazienza." Jessica smiled focusing her attention back to her work. "So, where were you last night?" she asked.

"Hmm. I had a job to take care off. The company needed an extra driver."

"Okay."

"Please don't kill yourself over this, Jess. Luca needs you and I need you, too." Alberto stood up heading for the door. "Love you, Jess."

"Love you too." Jessica muttered, but her words were shallow.

Once again, Jessica focused on her father's books, trying to create a plan on how to take back his empire, ignoring Alberto who stood for a few moments at the door watching her.

For the next few hours, Jessica vanished in her father's books. She didn't hear the keys jingle when Sofia came home with Luca. The boy ran straight to the office, hugging his mother. Jessica looked at him, hugging her tightly, hiding his little face inside her black dress.

"I'm home, Mommy." his voice came out suppressed as he pressed tighter against her leg.

"Hey sweetheart." Jessica rubbed his hair and then patted his back with a mother's loving touch. "Where's grandma?" Jessica asked and looking up seeing Sofia, standing at the door smiling. She was pleased by Luca's love for his mother.

"Hey, there she is. Go see what Alberto's doing in the kitchen. I'll be out in a second." she pushed him to tag along. Luca nodded and ran out. Sofia walked past Luca who ran passed her, taking a seat across from Jessica.

"Still not referring to him as father?" Sofia asked skeptically.

"He's not his father, Sofia. He only needs a male figure around, nothing more." She knew Sofia's words were sincere, but she couldn't give Alberto any more of her.

"So, how did it go today?" Jessica hurriedly changed the topic of the conversation.

"I met with Andrea Ambrosi. The capofamiglia of the Ambrossi family." Sofia said lowering her voice

"And?"

"He was more than happy to discuss further. What about Sabina?"

"She's with us."

"Just like that?"

"She needed a little persuading, but she hates the Saltinottis as much as we do. Maybe not more than she hates you." Jessica opened her desk's drawer, taking out a cigarette and lighting it up.

"That's understandable. My son killed her father and now I have to live with this eternal headache."

"What will we do now?" she asked Jessica waiting to hear her view.

"Now, we bring them all together here and plan what's next. We need to bring together the families before anything."

"And then?"

"Then we take them out, one by one."

"Who?"

"Anyone who doesn't go along with us. This way, we isolate the Saltinottis."

"About that..." Sofia paused. Jessica stopped and looked her.

"Andrea mentioned the new head of the Saltinottis. He's a crazy *Figlio di Puttana.*"

"Who?"

"Jacopo Saltinotti." A shiver climbed down Sofia's neck even by the sound of his name. Jessica looked surprised at Sofia whose face had turned black.

"Who's that?"

"He was a Soldato for the family and was never going to be consider representante because he was too reckless." Her body language showed that she knew more than just that.

"Reckless?"

"He's a lunatic, Jessica." Sofia crossed her hands over her chest.

"Why is he the head then?"

"Andrea said desperate times require desperate measures, whatever that means. That's what Andrea said."

"Do you think the Saltinottis are expecting us to return?"

"No. Not unless someone gave up our location. If they knew we were here, we'd already be dead."

"They wouldn't give us a single chance."

"Exactly. I wouldn't give us one."

"What are the Saltinottis currently up to?"

"I didn't discuss this with Andrea. You should ask him."

Jessica paused, drowning in her thoughts once again. The cigarette in her hand almost had turned to ash. She opened the drawer, took out another one and lit it up.

"Have Andrea and the other family heads come here in three days. I'll inform Sabina."

"So, is this final?"

"If we want to have a fighting chance…yes."

Sofia looked Jessica in the eyes and saw determination. The same determination - Francesco had in his eyes while trying to lead. It was the same determination - Luca and Michael had. This girl resembled Michael and Giovanni in appearance.

"I'll let them know right away. Get some rest, Jessica."

"I will, I promise." Jessica moaned looking at the books in front of her once again. There was no time for rest. Each minute that passes by was a step closer to her ultimate goal. It was time for action and she would sacrifice everything.

She opened her notebook and filled in the meeting's date, making sure she circled it in red. Until then, she needed to regain the trust of Sabina and prove worthy in her eyes.

## THE DINNER

For the next two days, Jessica spent most of her time inside her father's office. In the mornings, she drove Luca to school and came back home to study.

Jessica read her father's books repeatedly, like an accountant trying to go over a business' records. She found the names of all the families, studying in the detail about their history in New York City, tracing them back to Italy. Jessica also tried to identify the individuals that were now running the streets of New York by reading news articles as far back as two years. Her plan was to make the Empire City surrender to her family's control once again.

Order needed to be brought and Jessica believed more than ever that she was the one who could do it. Her fortitude and Sofia's expertise would lead the way.

Alberto spent most of his days outside at work,

allowing Jessica to work without any distractions. She was alone in the same spot where her father used to run the business. Now, she was now ready to run it by herself.

Sofia was out meeting with the family heads, laying the groundwork for what was about to come. After some scheduling delays and a week passing by, Jessica got ready to welcome the families inside her home where a traditional five-course Italian dinner would be held. The perfect opportunity to discuss business like before when her father, Luca was running things.

———

Jessica sat at the head of the table, glancing at the silvered cutlery. The house was filled with the smell of cooked food. The catering service she booked for the dinner was pricy, but it was worth it. She needed to leaved good impressions on her special guests.

Jessica grabbed one of the bottles of Santa Margherita Pinot Grigio DOC Valdadige and poured herself a glass, putting her cigarette in the ashtray. She counted the plates on the table. Six. Everything was set. The lights were dim and the old stereo playing Tarantella Napoletana from the kitchen.

She asked Alberto to take Luca out. She didn't want any interference during the most important night of her life.

A waiter came over offering her a glass of 1943 Giacomo Conterno. It left a soft burning feeling as she sipped away. That was the wine her father always used to close deals - a tradition of the Lombardi family.

"Everything ready?" Sofia entered the dining room, holding a half-empty glass.

"Yes." Jessica said, trying to hide her nervousness by taking a few more sips. She felt like she was going out on her first date.

"How do you feel?"

"Determined" was the only thing that escaped Jessica's lips.

"Good. You can't let them get to you."

"They won't."

"And I won't be able to help."

"I know Sofia. Don't worry."

"I trust you, Jessica. I wouldn't be here if I didn't." Sofia said finishing her wine and placing it on the table with a smile. Jessica smiled back, with reassurance.

The women spent the next half an hour in silence, like a family during a Christmas dinner, waiting anxiously for the guests to arrive. The waiters started bring the food to the table, placing the Aperitivo first. A wide variety of cured meat products and cheeses that would accompany the guests during the wine-drinking custom. They lit the candles and waited with their arms crossed behind their backs, looking straight ahead. True paisanos.

A few moments later the doorbell rang, echoing the whole house. One waiter opened the door and four sets of footsteps found their way to the dining room. Jessica and Sofia stood in position, waiting for the noble heads of the families to enter and take their seats.

Sofia rushed to the door to introduce the family heads as they entered the room. An old custom - the families had showing their appreciation to all those who would dine with the head of a household. Sofia cleared her throat as Andrea entered the room. "Andrea, head of the Abanos for over twenty years and a loyal friend." Sofia said warmly as Andrea gave his long black coat to one waiter, exposing his black suit and white shirt underneath it.

"It's a pleasure to meet Michael's bambina." Andrea said kissing her hand and slowly bowing before sitting at the other end of the table.

"Paolo Episcopo. Head of the Episcopos and a father to the Saint Peter Church of Manhattan." Sofia continued as a bald man entered, wearing a black ceremonial robe, with a large golden cross hanging around his neck. His eyes were lugged by black bags underneath, resembling a sick person, ready to collapse.

However, Jessica was startled by the man's appearance. Paolo looked stoic and calm, with a soft, loving smile. Under no circumstances, Jessica would suspect this man would be the head of a family.

The man walked in slow fearless steps and took a seat next to Andrea. "My pleasure, Signorina Jessica." The man spoke and bowed as he sat.

"Signorina…"

"She knows who I am." Sabina said averting her eyes

from Sofia as she walked in without introduction, taking a seat across from Paolo. Her maroon dress reflected a soft candlelight inside a dark room. Her face was covered in makeup, something that made it look worse. Her blonde hair was tied in ponytails while her backside was exposed.

Sofia cleared her throat, almost ashamed, sensing suspense in the air. She knew Sabina hated her and had every right in doing so. Sofia had a strong hunch that Sabina would make that clear if given the chance to speak.

Sofia extended her arm and raised her voice. "Julius Fondas. Head of the Fonda family and expert fixer." Sofia said as a man with gray hair entered the room. The man could barely walk, dragging along to take a seat next to Paolo. He looked older and sicker than Paolo, but he had an aura of success. His wrinkled skin didn't match his thick silver hair and exquisite taste in suits. He walked with the help of a cane and looked toward Jessica with his green eyes. Those eyes seemed discolored by the passage of time, like a dirty piece of glass.

He inspected and grinned acknowledging his appreciation and respect for her family. His eyes were like prism into the past, revealing not only his age, but his experience. Julius seemed like he had seen and knew more than anyone inside this room. Jessica already felt safe by Julius choosing to sit next to her. Jessica returned a warm grin and nodded to Sofia to take a seat next to Sabina.

Jessica sat between Sabina and Sofia. Sabina almost

turned her back to Sofia when she walked pass, but didn't when Jessica looked at her. Andrea looked troubled, but the rest seemed in good spirits.

"It's a pleasure to meet you all," Jessica said crossing her hands on the table as the waiters approached filling the guests' glasses with wine, then retreating. "It's been a long time since someone has gathered the families. Especially after the tragic events of the Bloodshed." Jessica continued.

"All the families are here but one." Andrea said in a joking manner.

"I don't believe the Saltinottis belong at this table anymore," Jessica said with a vicious smirk. Andrea nodded pleased with Jessica's claim and extended his hand, urging Jessica to continue. "Do we all agree on this?" Jessica asked in a strict tone trying to make sure there are no differences between the members present. Everyone nodded in agreement. Everyone but Julius who seemed suspicious.

"Why is that if I may ask?" Julius asked.

Jessica turned to him as silence dawned on the dining room. Julius and Jessica looked upon each other for a second and then she politely asked. "Do you disagree?"

"On the contrary. However, I would love to have all the facts, Signorina only."

"They declared a war on my family and the Giulianis." Jessica raised her voice, pointing towards Sofia. "They killed her son, her husband and my father is basically dead."

"But Francesco lit the fire of war." Julius continued staring at Jessica.

Jessica gasped and her hand squeezed the edge of the table, in a desperate attempt to keep herself calm. Her blood was boiling. How could this old man insult her like this? Come inside her home and mock her dead husband? Her lost love and all those who died by the hands of the Saltinottis. Jessica took a deep breath counting her words carefully. This moment was critical and would determine the fate of her family, her chance at success and revenge. She couldn't afford a single breakdown.

"I believe he did. But he was not in the boy-killing business." Jessica hissed and felt Sofia's hand on her leg. A mother's touch, that was a feeling of poise spread all over her body. Jessica's grip on the table relaxed. "But this is not the only reason they should not be allowed to be part of this." Jessica said smiling as she sought to regain control of the conversation. "Jacopo Saltinotti's out of control. Can we all agree on that?"

"I believe we can. Forgive me, Signorina. I just want to make sure that our actions are based on common sense. I like facts. Not false accusations." Julius said now smiling. Jessica's heart skipped a beat as she looked at his face. The man reminded her of her grandmother. Sometimes harsh but always for the best. She felt she could lean on this old man for advice.

Jessica took a sharp breath and continued. "Let's start with the Antipasto and discuss the details along the way.

Shall we?" Jessica raised her glass. The rest followed and drank in silence until they finished. The waiters stepped in again filling them and brought plates with the cheese.

"I believe we all know the reason for this meeting, but would you care to enlighten us Jessica?" Julius wanted to push the conversation forward, inviting Jessica to begin right away.

"With pleasure." Jessica said finishing her drink. Sofia nodded to the waiters to hurry and leave the room. A few moments of commotion and then silence. Everyone was waiting for Jessica to speak. Jessica lit a cigarette and took a drag, gathering her notes and ready to choose her words like an orator.

*"As Sabina and Andrea already know, we're back in business. I'm back in the game and made it my solemn duty to put an end to the depravity they call organized crime these days. I came back to regain what is rightfully ours not only for the Lombardis or Giulianis, but all the New York's Italian families. And this is the reason I gather you here this evening."*

The family leaders nodded pleased with Jessica and leaned closer wanting to hear every word. Jessica took another drag and let her cigarette rest on the ashtray. *"As of today, the Giuliani and Lombardi families are at war with all the petty gangs, street hustlers, the Saltinottis and the NYPD. We will not tolerate anyone messing with our businesses. I'm back to claim New York City as ours. Am I making myself clear?"*

Jessica said as she felt her blood pumping forcefully.

"If I may ask. Is there a plan in place, Signorina?" Julius asked concerned, but fascinated.

"Last week, I've spent countless hours studying everything from my father's detailed files. I know everything about you and the Saltinottis but very little about the small gangs that have surfaced in the last few years. Do you?" Jessica spoke as a lawyer who tries to persuade the jury. Everyone shrugged in bewilderment, including Julius. "You, Mr. Julius. You're a fixer. Shouldn't you know what our families are facing?" Jessica asked with satire, almost blaming him. Julius knew better than that and didn't consider her question as an insult.

"We've been out of the game for a while, Signorina Jessica. I know the ropes better than anyone, but my career ended because of the fallout after the Bloodshed." Julius admitted. He was excited to see the young daughter of Michael in front of him take his lead.

"Conosci il tuo nemico. Know thy enemy. That is what my father always said and you know it better than me." Jessica paused to take another drag as everyone nodded. Jessica saw Julius smile, giving her morale to continue. She stood up and walked inside the dining room with her cigarette in hand. Everyone waited in suspense, almost hanging from Jessica's lips.

"There's man named David." Jessica said after a long pause. "David Allen," she paused again waiting to see her guests' reactions.

"The head of the new organized crime unit?" Andrea exclaimed, unable to connect the pieces.

"Exactly."

"Our police insiders are gone. Don't even mention the FBI or CIA."

"They are gone for now, but not for long."

"Why do we need this guy, Jessica?"

"He's the key to our troubles. David will do the work for us while we idly stand by. The closer he gets to the core of these gangs, the stronger we get in the background."

Jessica was excited, but not everyone in the room shared the same spirit. "Are you crazy?" Sabina rebuked, unable to figure out Jessica's plan. "I don't work with Polizia."

"I didn't say we will work with him. He's committed to his vision of taking down criminals. Even if we wanted to put him on our payroll, it would be impossible. All we have to do is wait for him to discover all the Intel on the warehouses, the names of the ringleaders and their trade routes. When he does that, we will be a step ahead to seize everything he's targeting." Jessica said smiling, taking another drag and then putting it out while sitting back down.

Everyone in the room looked skeptical, thinking about Jessica's plan. Sofia looked with enlarged eyes, unable to believe Jessica had thrown the family minds in confusion rather than gaining their trust. Her proposal was a bit of a challenge.

"That needs lot of planning and inside contacts." Andrea argued with concern.

"I have everything planned, Andrea. You'll have one week to infiltrate the police department. Buy out the dirty cops and make some of your men start applying as police officers." Jessica answered confident in her presentation. "Our first target will be the Jamaicans, as promised to my lovely Sabina here. When they're out of the picture, we'll storm in and take another round of dirty cops as ours." Jessica winked to Sabina. "Does that sound solid to you?"

"Yes, definitely. The first week will be hard but dirty cops are like stray dogs. Begging for a new home. They'll get in bed with anyone."

"With that out of the way, Signor Paolo. I understand you are the head of the Church?"

"I prefer the term father, but yes."

"Have you ever been in the money laundering business?"

"No, I'm afraid not."

"Our accountant will show you the ropes. Your church will provide the perfect cover as our base of operation for the trade routes and laundering. We will make sure the churches gets their church taxes as always with a little extra."

Paolo nodded pleased with this scheme. Julius lifted his eyebrows. "That's actually a pretty good scheme, Jessica. How come you never thought of it, Paolo?" Julius pushed Paolo with his elbow laughing. The mood became milder and milder as every piece was falling into its place. Slowly, all present began trusting Jessica and the more she spoke, the more they committed.

"Sabina, you'll get the gun markets for now on and be responsible for supplying our families with ammunition."

Sabina nodded as she finished her glass of wine. Jessica fixed her eyes on Julius. "Signor Julius. I believe you know better than anyone what you have to do."

"Don't you worry, Donna Jessica. I know." Julius said grabbing her hand and kissing it. "Donna Jessica…" Paolo said as he got up, kneeling in front of her seat, kissing her hand with respect and recognition.

Jessica stared at Andrea, waiting for him to follow the example of the other family leaders. But Andrea stood there. "I'm not sure." He stuttered taking a quick breath. "I'm not sure if we can pull this off."

Sofia turned towards her old friend. He seemed certain a few days ago but now he was just there, lost. Sofia turned to Jessica looking worried.

But Jessica remained calm. She didn't even flinch. Jessica got up as Paolo sat down again. "What's the problem, Andrea?" Jessica asked softly but countering.

"It could all go to hell. If we don't succeed, we could all end up like your families." His voice trembled to the thought of the Bloodshed.

Paolo glanced from Sofia to Andrea and then at Jessica. "Signorina, Andrea's words has truth behind them. I'm siding with you but know a single mistake could send all of us to the afterlife." Paolo said making the sign of the cross. Jessica raised her arm to Paolo, commanding him to stop talking. Behind her eyes, there was fury. Jessica wasn't always that short-tempered but since the Bloodshed, her patience to others' fears had subsided. "Andrea." she said raising her voice, like a mother scolding her child.

"None of you are forced to join the alliance I"m proposing tonight. None of you are expected to join the new Italian empire that will be built inside the heart of New York City. The empire, I'll build back up with your lead. And I will not rule with friendship or love. I value respect and fear. So, mark my words. Anyone who doesn't side with me tonight, is against me and will have the same abode as the Saltinottis." Jessica was shouting and everyone stood still like time had frozen. Her speech was cut short as she coughed from smoking. Andrea was gripping the end of the table while Sofia was trying to diffuse her uneasiness by folding and unfolding a piece of the tablecloth. Where did this girl's power come from?

Andrea's body was shaking as he was battling his own vulnerabilities, worries and demons. "Fine, fine, fine" he said with a big exhale. He was almost out of breath. "I'm with you, Jessica Lombardi. I trusted your father, I trusted Luca and I'll trust you. He taught you well." He said coming to Jessica, kneeling to kiss her hand. Sofia let a long sigh of relief and stared at Jessica proudly. Suddenly, everyone felt certain around her, everyone honored her, even the most weak-hearted of them all, Andrea.

This moment for Jessica was significant. If Andrea refused, probably Paolo would, too. She needed them on her side and not against her. The waiters skipped the primo by guests' orders and began with the secondo.

Jessica went on, "I believe it is fair to offer everyone twenty percent of the profits. As I told Sabina, I'm not here for the profit. Is everyone fine with this?" Jessica asked hoarsely, talking as something was stuck in her throat. She tried drowning it with a long sip of wine. Everyone nodded and Paolo seemed more than pleased to the sound of Jessica's number. "If this is all, Buon Appetito and you are kindly dismissed afterwards." Jessica said coughing again. After twenty minutes or so, Sofia kindly ushered every family member to the door.

Jessica could hear the whispers between the family leaders, but her coughing made everything sound incoherent. She was only interested in the expressions of trust and appreciation especially from Andrea.

Jessica kept coughing, taking a linen napkin to cover her mouth. The coughing finally ceased, and she placed the napkin on the table, noticing a drop of blood in the middle. Jessica ignored it and folded it up, throwing it under one plate. She didn't want Sofia to know. There would be another long lecture of her pushing her to visit a doctor right away. Or another about how bad smoking is. Even her own mother didn't care so much.

A few moments later, Sofia returned to the room, as the waiters cleaned everything up from the table. Sofia had a bright smile; the same as a mother gives to her child when excelling at the exams. "You were amazing." Sofia said giving Jessica a soft warm hug.

"Thank you Sofia."

"Why didn't you fill me in with the plan?" Sofia complained.

"I wanted your feedback to be bona fide. Did I surprise you?"

"Well, you did."

"Do you think we got them?"

"I haven't seen such a blissful gathering since the days of your father."

"Really?"

"He was a natural talker."

"He had his ways sometimes. Should we worry about Andrea?"

"Andrea's loyal."

"Are you sure?"

"Absolutely. He's just afraid for his family. He has a son as well."

"He shouldn't be. That would be a liability."

"When you run things, make family a priority. It would appear as if you are their caretakers."

"I'll keep that in mind. Grazie, Sofia. I don't know what I'd do without you."

"You'll do just fine."

"Grazie Nonna…" Jessica said squeezing Sofia shoulder.

"I should get to bed. Big day tomorrow. You should too."

"I will." Jessica smiled as Sofia left the dining room.

Jessica remained at her seat, finishing the bottle of red wine that was left on the table, lighting another cigarette that drew her deeper in to her own dreams. She could feel the same ecstasy and numbness on her fingertips she felt before. She finally stood up for herself and her family's name. The families' leaders commitment proved she was a worthy heir to her father's empire and Francesco's. It was time to make New York bleed for what it did to her families.

## 10

## AT THE CINEMA

The lights were turned 0ff. Only but the sudden black and white flashes, coming from the huge screen at the end of the theater. The attendees were sitting silent, deafened only by the sounds coming from the theatre's speakers.

A gunshot and the theater flashed. The sound of police sirens coming out the speakers made it tremble. With popcorn in their hands, the moviegoers were shocked to miss the next scene. It was so intense nobody took their eyes off the screen. Except for one fat man.

The fat man was sitting on seat 3C, dressed with a top hat and a long trench coat. He wasn't there for entertainment. He didn't care about police men hunting down gangsters. Already, he lived that life, and the movie was filled with exaggerations.

The fat man arrived during the middle of the flick even though he had his seat reserved a week earlier. He made himself comfortable before leaning closer to talk to a man sitting in seat 3B. Another set of gunshots boomed. *You're surrounded.* The sound from the speakers smothered the fat man's words.

"Any word on…?"

The man in the 3B turned his head with a subtle motion, like he had no idea who the fat man was. He took a sip from his drink, making the sucking sound. His soda was nearly empty. "How did you know I'd be here?" the man asked curiously but worried. "We know everything. Any word on…?" the fat man repeated.

"Six families are meeting this evening. They're planning something big." the man said facing the screen.

"What are they planning?" the fat man asked losing patience.

"I don't know yet." the man shrugged feeling a gun pointed from the back of his seat.

"You know what this is, right?" the fat man asked him angrily. The man in the front seat nodded yes.

"Tell me what they are planning or you'll be part of this fucking movie?"

"I told you I don't know yet. I'm still gathering details." the man whispered as the sounds from the speakers played music, unable to silence their voices.

"You have 24 hours or else." the fat man told him getting up from his seat and leaving.

A black Cadillac with tinted windows was waiting for him outside the theatre. He got in the back seat and it drove off speeding into the night.

## 11

## NAILING THE HARPOONS

**D**avid heard his alarm clock ringing. The annoying sound rang thrice before he pressed the off-button. He got up, wearing nothing but boxers. *Thursday, 5:02* - time to get out of bed.

David showered as his coffee machine was brewing Folgers' Breakfast Blend. Once out of the bathroom, he warmed up a chicken sandwich he had from the night before and poured himself a cup.

The agent's apartment was kept tidy. There were no decorations and everything was white from the tables to the walls. No one visited, but if they did, they would think his place resembled a mental institution.

David sat at the table and grabbed one of the police reports lying in front of him. Every morning, David had the same routine before he got ready for his day of work. The file named 'Gun Traders of New York' caught his attention. The case file listed Jamaican gun smugglers' names and rumored hideouts as well as CI statements, arrest histories and other documented crimes.

He kept studying, always coming across in the name; *Hatchet.* Possibly a codename. David spent the rest of his time at home trying trying to find out any connections with other gun-running operations and smuggling rings.

David pushed the file to the side and performed a search in the CIA's database on the name 'Hatchet'. A few seconds later, a name popped up - *Kynami 'Hatchet' Williams.*

Kynami had over thirteen arrests and spent five years in prison. He was out on the streets and though the gun smuggling led to him in the past, there was nothing recent to go on. David finished his sandwich and searched for Kynami's financial records but few leads popped up. It took over two and half hours and a few calls to his colleagues in DC get what he was looking for.

Over the next few hours, David became familiar with the organized crime cases since the Bloodshed. The trail of Italian families had gone cold after the leading members of the Giulianis and the Lombardis were sitting in jail or killed. Their assets were liquidated as the surviving members of both families wanted to rid them-selves of anything tying them to organized crime in the last five years.

David found out Kynami had business contracts with some empty shell companies that bought and sold the assets of the Lombardi Family and Associates after the police's confiscation of the "Otter Bank." The Otter bank served clients with a minimum of a million dollars in assets and granted offshore accounts to Michael Lombardi and associates. A man by the name of Jonathan Hatchet was now moving huge sums of money through that bank on a weekly basis. Coincidentally, a warehouse near the docks which was owned by Michael Lombardi and Associates appeared to be listed as Kynami Hatchet's property since 1996.

David closed the file smiling. This was a stretch but a great place to start. What he had here would it had been enough to get a judge to grant a search warrant for that warehouse?

David got up to wash dishes, looking at the clock. *09:50 AM.* In ten minutes, the hired taxi scheduled to take him to work would be waiting outside. David got dressed quickly and headed out.

———

Thirty-five minutes later, David enter the 7th precinct. The officers saluted him; some respectfully, while others smiling with mockery. David ignored them, go up the curving marble stairs in the station's middle, leading directly to his office.

Once inside, he looked at his desk. It was exactly as he left it the day before. He grabbed the phone and dialed the number of the precinct's captain and second in-charge. "Captain Rogers, come to my office right away. I have something to discuss with you." David said quickly hanging up before dialing another number. "Agent Miles, my office in five." he said with authority and hung up, not waiting for Mile's response. David opened his files, organizing the important points he jotted down earlier in the morning.

Two minutes later, the bald-headed captain entered the room, holding a coffee mug in his hand, followed by a clean-shaven man, wearing a black suit that matched David's.

David signaled for the men to sit down. "Captain Rogers and Agent Miles." he said turning over his notes, pushing copies forward towards them. Miles combed his slick black hair to the back, ready to speak, but he stayed silent as Captain Rogers took the lead. "Did you come up with all this by yourself, Special Agent Allen?" the captain asked, not believing that someone could come up with a solution to their dilemma so fast.

"Today in the morning." David said sharply. "I spoke with the DA on the way here. He's willing to get us a search warrant by the evening." He raised his glance on Miles.

"Agent Miles. I want the task force ready for the evening. Is that clear?" David commanded.

"Yes, sir. I'll get on it right away." Miles said getting up, leaving Captain Rodgers and David.

"This is the result of proper detective work, Captain." David said as the door closed. "It's ABC police 101. Your men could have got it done in hours if they weren't busy taking bribes from the criminals." he said giving a stern look to Rodgers.

Captain Rodgers appeared upset. "For the millionth time, Special Agent Allen, my officers are not on any criminals' payrolls."

"Then you are either blind or being bribed as well, Captain. Everything is as clear as day."

"We do not have the fancy trainings like you boys out wherever you are from, Agent Allen."

"But you did, Captain. If I recall, Quantico a few years."

"Are you implying something, Special Agent Allen? If yes, say it straight to my face."

"Not at all, Captain. I do know you're running a corrupt police force. "

"For the last time Agen-"

"I know. Your officers are model citizens and blah blah blah. Anyway, I will not hand over any information on this investigation to you or your cops until we have finished. I'll keep you briefed out of courtesy for your dedication to this country, but nothing more." David said shifting his attention back to the case files, organizing them neatly in a pile.

The captain stood up speechless. He couldn't believe a man who spent three days in his precinct was now running it. To Captain Rodgers, David was a man who spent a few hours behind a desk and now, he believes he is the best detective in the world.

"Mister Allen…"

"Captain Rodgers, It's Special Agent Allen. Now that you know my title correctly, you're dismissed."

"Please, do not work on this case by yourself."

"I'm not Thomas Miller, Captain Rodgers. I'm familiar with his past achievements and dedication. It was a flaw that the FBI allowed him to go rogue. But I know ultimately that you guys failed him."

"I'm afraid you'll end like him, Special Agent. That's my worry."

David's eyes flinched.

"Captain. I was assigned with a simple task that has a simple solution. Agent Miller went rogue. I'm a professional and my work is far beyond the scope of this local police department. If you can excuse me, Captain I have work to do. Unlike the rest of this department."

"Very well, Special Agent." the Captain said putting on his hat. "Keep me briefed. We can give you all the support you need." he said closing his door behind with worrisome written on his face.

David returned to his work like the conversation with Captain Rodgers never had taken place. He opened his desk drawer taking out Agent Miller's file; a thick file with many colorful identifiers attached. He opened it staring at Miller's picture on the first page. "I won't be like you." he mumbled clutching Miller's picture. "I'll show everyone you didn't deserve the Medal of Valor.

Neither you or the *'so-called cop hero'* Garcia." David spat, almost underlining the word *hero*, and dropped the file back inside his drawer.

Tomorrow, the Jamaican guns would be off the streets of New York for good.

**12**

———

## BLACKMAILED

Andrea was sitting on a bench in Central Park holding a large loaf of *Filone di Renella*, dressed in a long black trench coat, with a hat that shaded his eyes. He cut off small pieces, throwing them on the cold ground. A few moments later, the pigeons came swarming in, scrambling to eat.

The temperature was getting colder as the sun hid behind the dense foliage of the trees. Children were playing with their parents in the park's play area.

The crunching sound of grass got louder behind Andrea but he didn't turn around. He already knew who it was as a man's cane was clicking.

The older man took a seat next to Andrea, fixing his grey scarf.

"Buonasera, Julius."

"Andrea."

"You took your time getting here."

"I was busy."

"I've been waiting in this cold weather for almost an hour."

"There's a café across the street. Why didn't you get something to warm you up?"

"I see you have jokes, my friend. Anyway, what do we have, Julius?"

"Tony Miles."

"Who is he?"

Julius handed him a file with the agent's name written on the divider. "See for yourself."

Andrea opened the file. His cold hands were trembling and his fingertips were getting numb. "Tony's second in command?"

"That's right."

"He's high up on the task force."

"Keep reading."

"He's decorated, blah blah blah."

"Keep going."

"Oh. Melina and Bartholomew Miles."

"Essato!"

"Where do they live?"

"Next page."

Andrea turned the page and saw a series of photos of Melina and Bartholomew at a mansion with a pool.

"California?"

"Apparently, Agent Tony Miles lives here alone. But that doesn't stop us from paying his family a visit, does it?"

"Great work, Julius. I shall pay a visit to Signore Miles later this evening."

"Glad, I could assist."

"What about the cops?"

"Turning our attention to the Jamaicans would make the matter easier as Donna Jessica proposed."

"I see Jessica's learned a lot from her father."

"Let's all hope so." Julius said grunting as he got up on his cane and walked away. Andrea stood alone, holding Agent Miles' file and called his soldatos to prepare for the evening.

———

Tony Miles was driving down the street in his black Sedan, feeling the heat coming out of his car's air conditioning system. The hot air made him feel dizzy, almost putting him to sleep. He turned it off to stay focused on the road and wasn't driving fast.

Behind him, was another black Sedan that tailed him from the precinct. As the man in charge of the strike team, David Allen was followed at all times. It was mandatory that no member of David's task force be left unsupervised. Though many believed David cared about their integrity, Tony knew David was paranoid as fuck. He cared more about not being betrayed than his officers.

Miles slowed down once he reached the outside of his home, rented by the FBI. He pressed the button inside his car and the front gate opened, revealing a grand courtyard with a small pool in the back. Tony slowed down before reaching the driveway which was under the shadow of the two-story building.

The Black Sedan that trailed him parked and the men inside had their lunches unpacked. Miles waved at them while they waved back. They were ordered to be on-guard for the night.

Miles walked up the gravel driveway, heading towards the front entrance of the house. It would have been a great place for him and family. Unfortunately, his work was too dangerous for them to stay with him especially during the Task Force's purge. He pressed the code to open the main door. *9-2-2-4* and the door opened with a click.

The house had the most sophisticated home security system. Over ten cameras, covering almost every square inch. There were three separate alarm systems and a safe room with guns and rations that could last for months. *A generous package by the boys in blue.*

Miles closed the door behind him and hung his keys beside the door. He noticed something was out of place, so he inspected the living room. By instinct, he grabbed the gun from his waist. The second alarm system had been turned off. Miles loaded his weapon and crept towards the staircase. His footsteps were muted by the grey carpet's lining. He reached the staircase, but found nothing.

Tony swiftly focused back on the living room and the

area leading to the kitchen. He ducked between the television set and coffee table like an animal hunting its prey, Once he reached the kitchen to investigate, that's when he heard the sound of a gun being loaded right behind him. "Don't move." a man said in a heavy accent.

Miles felt cold sweat dripping down from his face. His white uniform shirt was soaking wet. "Drop it." the man said and Miles followed his orders. He placed the weapon slowly on the floor and raised his hands.

The man patted him. "He's clean, Boss." the man shouted pushing Miles forward into the middle of the kitchen.

All of the lights in the kitchen were suddenly turned on and the place was lit up, revealing three men standing behind a plastic table. One of them took a seat at the table while the others were clutching their guns. The man sitting at the table gestured to Miles to take a seat.

Miles sat across from the man. "Sono Andrea." the man said with a gigantic smile. Miles felt like he wanted to vomit.

"I believe you know who I am. You guys are in a load of shit. I'm the fucking police." Miles growled.

"We know who you are, Agent Tony Miles. However, do you know why I'm here?" Andrea said in a heavier Italian accent than he normally spoke. He had found out that accent was used to send a message back in the day and it was time to bring that message back.

"No, I do not."

"Chula Vista. 4th Avenue and Mankato St. Does it ring a bell, Agent?"

Miles remained silent. The man in back of him then punched him. *"Answer when your boss asks you a fucking question."* The lights were on but Miles' life was getting darker.

"Stay with me, Signore Miles."

"Yes. I know the street." he answered.

"Bene."

"What do you want from me, then?"

Andrea threw a copy of the file that Julius handed him a few hours ago on the table. But there were only pictures of Miles's child and wife. "Take a closer look to make sure I'm not mistaken."

Miles picked up the file, fearing that something happened to his family. He opened it seeing pictures of his son playing at school and of his wife at the gym. Then, another punch landed on Agent Miles.

*"Fuck!* What do you want?" Miles repeated faintly, unable to hold in the pain.

"The Jamaicans? When?"

"Is my family safe?"

"They are for now, Miles. But that depends on you."

"Depends on what??"

"It depends on how, Agent Miles. That's what matters right now. The Jamaicans. Give me everything you know on them. There's a raid. When?"

"T—omorrow night."

"Where?"

"A warehouse on Agnes and E 17th street."

"Who's warehouse? Give me a name."

"Kynami 'Hatchet' Williams"

"Grazie Tante, Tony. We appreciate your help."

"Please. Don't hurt my wife and son."

"As long as you keep cooperating with us, Signore Miles, we have no reason to."

"I gave you what you want."

"Consider this the beginning of a great relationship, Agent Miles."

Miles pressed his face against his palms, unable to fathom what had just happened. His sweat got colder with every word the man said. Now Agent Miles was powerless as the next criminal.

"By the way, make sure you refrain from sharing this conversation of ours this evening. I know you will, right?"

"Y-yes."

"Should I mention what will happen at the zoo they love so dearly if you don't?"

"No. Please. You have my word."

"*E stato un piacere* which means Agent Miles, it's a pleasure." Andrea got up and nodded to the man behind Miles. The man took out the bullets in Miles' gun and throw it a few feet away.

"We'll be in touch." Andrea said departing with his three Soldatos.

David sat alone inside the kitchen in silence for the next few minutes. He then got up and headed to the bathroom to vomit like a man who is seasick. His face was pale and he was shaking uncontrollably. The OC Task Force's case was just hijacked by the fucking Italians.

Miles laid on the carpet in the living room as tears were running down his face. He loosen his tie and didn't know if how he would be able to fix this.

## 13

# BLOODSHED AT THE CONSTRUCTION SITE

The race to reclaim New York had begun and there was no moment to relax, not until Jessica Lombardi proved herself worthy. She had to show she was capable of leading not only to herself but to the Dons of the Italian families, the criminal Saltinottis, law enforcement, and even to her son, Luca.

Jessica went over the finances she would hand over to the Episcopos. She needed to make sure that everything was in order before handing over the financial books of her entire operation. It was a risky move. If the Episcopos sided with the Saltinottis, it would destroy her entire operation. As a sign of good faith, Jessica worked with full transparency. They saw a glimpse of her rage at the meeting. The Lombardi Family had the backing of some of the most dangerous hit men in the history of New York City.

Everything was in order. Most of the family's old assets had been confiscated, but that would change soon. She closed the books and prepared to review some last points on strategy when there came a knock on the door. "Entrare" she said fixing her eyes ahead, lighting a cigarette. Jessica could use a break.

Alberto entered the room appearing sad. "Smoking again?"

"Nasty habit. I can't help it."

"There's a man to see you, amore mio."

"Send him in."

"Right away, Donna."

"Oh and Alberto…"

"Hmm?"

"*Grazie di tutto.*" Jessica said with a tiny look of affection in her eyes. A tiny flash of love that made Alberto smile. Jessica wasn't always like that and Alberto appreciated every moment he could get from her. "For what?"

"Just send him in, tesoro."

Alberto bashfully left the room. A few moments later, a man entered the room, dressed in a black trench coat and a black hat. He removed it as he came inside, revealing his messy curly black hair. "Donna Jessica." he said in a deep voice filled of respect.

"Sì?"

"Andrea sent me."

Jessica leaned further on the desk and took a drag from her cigarette. "Close the door and take a seat, please.

"We have a name and location on the Jamaicans."

"We have many locations on the Jamaicans. I want the main one."

"Our men know where the main headquarters are located." the man said expecting Jessica's response.

"Then, tell me." Jessica was furious that the man was not getting to the point.

"I'm sorry, Donna. Tomorrow evening, the new task force will be raiding it which is at Agnes and E 17th Street."

"That used to be our warehouse."

"I know, Donna Jessica. A man named Kynami acquired it after your father's liquidation."

"Kynami?"

"Sì."

"Listen carefully. Tell Julius that I want him to tip off Kynami tonight that the task force raids."

"Why would we do that?"

"We need him to move everything before he loses everything. He will be forced to use his other warehouses."

"But we already know his main location?"

"Exactly. He'll be expecting the strike tomorrow. If we strike tonight, when he has everything packed and ready to move, it will save us time and things will go unnoticed."

"Si, Donna Jessica."

"Consult with Julius first. If he gives the okay, let me know. I'll come down there myself. Go now!"

The man almost jumped out of his chair and ran down the hall, heading out the door. Alberto was still standing at the doorstep. "Are you sure this is a good idea?"

"It's an excellent one, Alberto."

"No, I mean heading down there."

"I'm not my father. They need to see I'm in charge."

"Are you Francesco?" Alberto blurted out mistakenly. It was hard for him to deal with a woman living in the past. Jessica had a bright future ahead of her, but lately, she was living in the former.

"No. Francesco was reckless. I'm Donna Jessica, Alberto."

Alberto chuckled. "You're right, cuore mio."

"Don't worry. I'll take care of everything. I think I should get ready."

"Be careful, Donna. Do that for me, please…and Luca." Alberto said as he left.

Jessica stood there for a moment, reflecting on her husband's words. He loved her and most of the time, he was right. Back in Italy, his family was part of the mafia, but Alberto never was exposed to what Jessica and Francesco experienced.

———

Later that evening, Jessica Lombardi was a few blocks away from the Kynami's warehouse. Julius was standing alongside her with Andrea. They were dressed in black leather coats with furs as the wind blew hard as forecasted.

The road in front of them was closed off with a yellow tape and orange cones. Construction workers were coming and going in trucks throughout the area. The air was filled with the constant buzzing of machinery and equipment moved and loaded.

The rest of the place was dark with no light posts on the street. Everyone was fast asleep except for the workers. There were only the orange lights emerging from the trucks. "Construction, this late, huh?" Jessica said sarcastically.

"Kynami disguises his gun shipments behind all of this construction work. Smart, I have to admit." Julius told her, rubbing his hands together.

"Yes, indeed." Jessica lit up a cigarette as the three of them stood on the side of the road, like three people waiting to take a taxi home.

"No matter, your plan is brilliant, Donna Jessica. We'll grab the trucks and take them back to Paolo warehouses to sell off for charity. A generous offering for Paolo and the Church." Andrea said patting Jessica on the shoulder like a father showing his appreciation to his daughter.

"Where did he get the money for empty warehouses?"

"They are abandoned church dumps. The police

doesn't even bother with what belongs to the clergy," Julius replied.

Jessica took another few puffs and threw the cigarette on the ground. It was a smart move having Paolo Episcopo as a partner.

"Is Sabina coming?" Andrea asked a little worried. The man who extorted the FBI agent was fond of his new Donna. He was always a boss-inside-the-office type, having his men do his dirty work.

"Yes. She's on her way with our men." Jessica pointed out. "I sent someone over there to check and made sure she's safe."

The three waited for another few minutes as the construction trucks kept going up and down the narrow street. Jamaican gangsters, dressed as construction workers kept loading the trucks with boxes of weapons making sure that his warehouse was clear before tomorrow evening.

The screeching of car tires were heard and moments later, three black Cadillacs flew through the dark street. Italian Soldatos, carrying Thompsons, got out off the cars. The men were wearing black leather trench coats, covering their faces with kevlars underneath their coats.

Sabina inspected the men, followed by Sabina, Andrea and Julius. "I can't believe they will fall for the bait," Jessica said like a little girl pulling a silly prank.

"Yes, they will." Julius said looking at the Jamaicans working. "Everyone's ready?"

"Si!" Sabina said taking out her Colt 45. A gift from her father when she was fifteen.

"Let's go." Jessica said grabbing her Smith and Wesson Model 19. She checked her bullets and smiled. The smirk of a leader, ready to take down her rival.

Jessica walked in front, followed by Sabina and the men, as Julius and Andrea stayed behind for backup with five men, monitoring the operation by phone.

The Italians move quickly down the street where the warehouse was located. They unloaded their Thompsons and after thirty seconds, the men were laying in pools of blood.

The street was clear. Everyone reloaded before moving closer, taking cover behind the slabs.

From inside the warehouse, more Jamaicans came out, firing AR-15s. Others came out to the street but were ambushed quickly. The rapid gunfire exchanges filled the night. This normally silent street was tonight's war zone.

Jessica wandered into an alleyway next to the warehouse, hiding behind a series of green dumpsters. She knew the warehouse's layout from the map that her father left in his office. Jessica drifted inside the warehouse, leaving her guard behind and headed for the stairs on the side of the building which led straight to Kynami's office.

Fifty feet behind her, the gunshots kept falling like rain. The Jamaicans seemed to shrink in number. Jessica looked behind and saw two of her men lying on the ground hit about ten yards away. *Casualties of war for a greater cause as they were dying serving their Boss.*

Jessica reached a discolored rusty door at the end of the staircase and peaked inside Kynami's office. She saw a man with dreadlocks, extending to his waist. He was crouching over a large safe, throwing bags of money inside green duffle bags. Jessica ran in and ducking behind an old metal desk, hiding from Kynami.

The moment he heard the door open, he turned around and shot his Uzi, leaving over twenty bullet holes inside the door. Jessica heard him panting and cursing. The man was petrified and was caught off guard. All of Kynami's weapons were boxed up ready to go to the other warehouse. He didn't have enough to defend his warehouse from this attack.

Kynami lowered his gun trying to find the person who was hiding inside his office. Jessica could hear his creeping steps behind the desk. He moved a leather chair a few feet away from the desk, with the room's library on his backside. The office was lit up only by a dim light. Kynami removed the Uzi's magazine to reload.

There was Jessica's chance. She got up and two deafening shots echoed the hallow office, followed by Kynami's scream. Her ears buzzed and for a moment, Jessica lost her balance. Everything became blurry for a moment when she got up seeing Kynami leaning against the bookcase bleeding. His Uzi fell a few feet away from him. Jessica pointed her gun at him. "Save it, Kynami," she said with rage in her eyes which looked like two dark holes as she stood under the lamp.

"Who are you?" the man said with a heavy accent; his words coming out muddled through his grunts of pain.

"You're in my warehouse, Kynami."

"I don't know you lady."

Kynami tried reaching for his gun but another gunshot made him freeze.

"I'm Jessica Lombardi. Does the name sounds familiar?"

"The Lombardis are all dead."

"No, they are not."

"I have money. Take it. Take my guns."

"No, Kynami. You see. I'm not here for your money or guns alone."

"What then?"

"I'm here to take back what's mine."

Jessica walked with slow intimidating steps closer to him. She sat on the edge of his desk, looking at her gun as if she didn't care. Kynami was terrified of what would happen next. Jessica saw sweat running profusely down his face. He had trouble swallowing.

"Tonight, you will die, Kynami."

"Do what you have to do. It's not only me in this town. The Jamaicans will come after you when they hear I'm dead."

"I hope they do. You should be honored. You'll be the first martyr of my crusade."

The vengeance boiling inside her for so long had suddenly taken form. Now, she was in the driver's seat.

"Any last words?"

"God help y-"

A gunshot interrupted his words as his head exploded by the bullet. Jessica stood there motionless afterwards, still pointing at his head. The buzzing returned but this time she shook it off like a skilled veteran. The first kill for Jessica Lombardi. She inhaled the warehouse-'s copper smell and deemed herself worthy of bearing the names of Lombardi and Giuliani.

Jessica stood up and gathered the duffle bags of money Kynami had left behind. She placed them over her shoulders and walked down the iron staircase, heading towards the street.

When she reached the construction trucks, the place looked like a scene from a macabre horror movie. Blood and bodies were everywhere. Sabina was standing next to a construction truck checking out her weapon as Andrea and Julius were walking closer to the scene.

"Everything okay?" Andrea asked with his hand inside his pockets, trying to hide the shaking of his body. Jessica dropped the bags on the ground revealing stacks of hundred-dollar bills inside. She took out a few packs and handed them to Julius and Andrea. "Give the men something for their hard work this evening."

Consider this the first of many," Jessica said placing her gun back in her purse looking like an empress who had just conquered a city. Julius bowed respectfully. "Of course, Donna." he said as he and the men turned around to inspect the scene for any last remnants.

"It went far better than I expected Jessica," Sabina admitted looking around. "What's the plan now?" she asked handing a bag of money to the huge man behind her who threw it in one of the Cadillacs.

"We pull out. The police mustn't know we were here." Jessica said thinking aloud.

"We can put this on the Jews." Julius shouted from the other side of the truck as it moved closer.

"How about that! Brilliant idea!"

"I'll handle it." Julius said nodding to two of his men who ran out of Kynami's office to retrieve the rest of the money and other contraband .

"I trust you, Julius and Andrea, with my life. It's your chance to take over this this city's police precinct."

"For sure, Donna Jessica. we're working on it already."

"Today was a success, but this war is far from over. We'll be in touch. Andrea keep me updated. Sabina talk with Paolo. He knows what to do." Jessica closed heading for her car, victorious. All nodded in agreement.

The Jamaicans' trucks were on their way to Paolo's warehouses and the three martyrs from Jessica's army were removed from the scene and secretly buried in one of Paolo's church cemeteries overnight. Sabina's men made sure that there was no evidence left at the scene implicating the Italians.

Jessica returned home, tired. The first strike was a

success and for the foreseeable future, New York would follow in similar fashion, bringing it to its knees. The feeling of victory Jessica would never let die. It was the first night she felt as close to Francesco since the Bloodshed. She could feel him watching her every move.

**14**

---

## HEAD NO MORE

Amelia was sleeping in a twin-size bed, covered in a big heavy blanket. Her bedroom's window was open, letting in a soft breeze. That breeze bounced off the heat from the inside the home.

She was tossing and turning, struggling to find a comfortable position. The sound of the doorbell echoed from the first floor up to her room, further disrupting her sleep. The second ring caused her son, Anansi to cry which echoed the first floor. Amelia opened her eyes and sat up. "Kynami?" she uttered removing the blanket.

The cry of her baby kept getting louder. Amelia felt that something wasn't right. She looked at the bed again and didn't see her husband, Kynami. Once again he was out working late again with his construction company. That's the excuse he told her which was true and false.

Amelia got up and ran to the next room, picking up young Anansi, rocking him left and right, shushing him.

With the baby in her arms, Amelia walked down the stairs to the first floor. The house was silent and everyone in the neighborhood was sound asleep. "Kynami? Did you forget your keys again," Amelia gasped when she saw his keys on the kitchen counter.

Suddenly, she started breathing heavily worried as if something wasn't right. The clock above the stove read: *05:30 AM*.

Amelia walked towards the window and peeked out the blinds. There was no one outside. "Kynami?" she called trembling while her hand rested on the door handle. With her baby in her arms, she opened the front door. On the doorstep, lied an old carton, with her name written on it - *Amelia Williams*.

She paused, trying to figure out why someone would leave her a box this late at night. *Was it a joke?* Amelia walked back inside, putting Anansi inside his crib. Then, she went back to the front, picking up the box.

It felt heavier than it looked. Amelia was afraid to bring it inside, so she opened it and a loud scream shook the entire neighborhood. A cry of desperation filled the airwaves. The neighbors' porchlights suddenly came on one by one.

The carton fell to the ground as Amelia hid her face inside her hands. Kynami's head rolled out, rolling down the stone stairs into the street. "Kynami! No! Why?"

Amelia screamed. Her baby, terrified by its mother's screams, started crying uncontrollably. In a matter of seconds, the neighbors came out in groups to witness the unspeakable tragic death of Kynami 'Hatchet' Williams.

## 15

## THERE'S A MOLE

Agnes street was blocked off with yellow police tape at both ends. It was a dull morning; dark gray clouds covered the sunlight, painting the entire city monochrome.

David walked between the reporters trying to get good photos of the scene and interviews from the detectives. David shoved his way through the camera flashes which disrupted the dullness, making the place appear like the red carpet entrance to the Grammys. However, there was no red carpet; only a road full with the blood of Jamaicans.

The crime scene was full with police officers, FBI, ATF and CIA agents canvasing, taking statements from witnesses in the area, trying to find the needle in the haystack. David walked under the yellow tape and put his plastic gloves on, preparing to inspect the crime scene's gruesomeness. David stopped before doing so and took a deep breath.

Earlier, a call woke him up around 04:30, ruining his good sleep. It was from the Captain Rodgers telling him to get to the crime scene as soon as possible. Two hours later, the man was standing in the middle of a New York battlefield. Almost a day before he was set to order his strike team to raid this warehouse and disband the Jamaicans for good, someone was quicker and deadlier than he was.

David walked between the bodies and inspected the old warehouse that had more holes in it than Swiss cheese. He stood there checking out the building with a single thought in his mind; there's a mole in his unit. Everything had been silent until the moment he made headway and now everything had suddenly turned into a huge pile of trash.

As he stood there thinking over the matter, Agent Miles approached him. He had the look of a man, who had grown ten years older in one night. David sighed when he noticed the dark bags under Miles' eyes and sweat pouring down his face.

"What happened here, Agent?" David ordered.

"We don't know, sir," Miles stuttered fixing his hair.

"What's got into you, Agent Miles? You look like shit this morning."

"I had a terrible night, sir. I was sick, and I got called in way earlier."

"Fill me in here, first and then go get some rest."

"Witnesses in the area said they heard gunshots, by the count of them, hundreds. They stayed away fearing that they would get caught in the crossfire."

"I can see that. Do we have a motive and suspicion on who was behind the attack?"

"No one knows. There are only Jamaicans that are dead, sir."

"No other casualties?"

"None so far. We're waiting for forensics to return the tests from the blood lab to determine, sir."

David stood there even more disgusted than before. His morning routine was broken and someone ruined his plan on taking out the Jamaicans. Now, he's back to zero in his investigation. Miles kept talking but David wasn't paying attention. David couldn't hear anything coming out from Miles' mouth. It was moving like an old silent flick.

"A-anything else, sir?"

"No. Got get some rest, Agent Miles."

Miles walked beside David releasing a long sigh of relief, feeling vomit pressing his throat, trying to erupt.

"Oh, and Agent Miles." David said still examining the warehouse's exterior.

Agent Miles paused turning around nervous, "Yes, sir?"

"I believe it's not a coincidence that a mysterious band of bandits attacked tonight. I think we may have a mole in our unit."

"Mole? How, sir?"

"I don't know. Did you give details to the strike team yesterday about today's raid?"

"Yes, sir. I did after you ordered me to brief them."

David turned around disgusted like a mother ready to scold her child. "Agent Miles, I don't have to tell you that this was very incompetent. I said brief to prepare, not tell them. From now on, the strike teams will only be informed moments before the raid. Go home and rest. When I'm done with this investigation, we'll perform background checks on everyone in the department including the captain. Am I clear?"

"Yes, sir." Miles said walking away fast, pushing away the reporters until he reached the other side of the street. He ran there and gripped an iron trash can. The moment his hands touched it, the vomit came out like a volcano.

David kept walking through the crime scene and knew there would be very few leads there. Whoever is behind this are professionals. They didn't leave any clues behind. From the Jews to the Italians, anyone could have done this. David took a long look around and then walked inside the warehouse.

The crime scene inside was as brutal as the exterior. Bodies were everywhere. Nothing but bullets and dead men. The walls had huge shelves which appeared to emptied. David spotted a woman possibly in charge of the forensics and went up to her, trying to avoid stepping on the bodies.

"Excuse me. Miss.?" David said standing with his

arms crossed behind his back. The woman wearing a blue police jacket written with the word *'forensics'* on its back and the blonde hair looked up, giving her full attention to her notes in her hands.

"Yes?"

"Special Agent David Allen. Head of the Organized Crime Task Force."

"Mariah Jones. How can I help you, Agent?"

"Do we have any clues on what was stolen?"

"From what we know from before, perhaps only military-style weapons. That's what's in the police logs from previous searches."

"Just that?"

"A safe in Kynami's office was left open on the second floor. You might want to take a look, Special Agent." The woman said with a horrified look on her face.

"Why is that?"

"I haven't been up there yet, sir. I just heard…"

"Heard what?"

"Have a look for yourself, sir."

David looked around, spotting the stairs leading to Kynami's office. "Inform the Captain, I'm here, Jones." David said as he ran up the rusty squeaking iron stairs to Kynami's office. When he entered, the smell of copper filled his nostrils.

The whole room was a mess; the room was shot up, the safe left open and a headless body lying in a gigantic island of blood. A few detectives were moving around inside, taking pictures of the scene, archiving everything they could find. Everything was marked, except for the body.

David took a step closer and could feel his stomach rumbling, spinning like a washing machine. The headless body of Kynami was lifeless on the ground. His right hand was cut off lying a few feet away from a gun which appeared that he was reaching for. It could be anyone's, but something inside David told him that it belonged to Kynami. This execution was a message sent to the rest of the rivals in the city. *A new player is in town.*

David crouched a few feet away from the body and took a closer look. There were bullets inside his legs. The bookcase behind him was splattered with blood. He kept inspecting when he heard someone behind him clear his throat. "Gentlemen. Leave the room." David heard the voice of the Captain Rodgers and turned around swiftly.

"Captain."

"Special Agent Allen." the Captain said with a look of frustration on his face.

"Captain, this is a huge mess."

"I know David."

"Special Agent Allen."

"I know your name. My men were given orders not to touch the body until you arrived."

"Clean cut. Blood on the bookcase. The head and right hand removal were postmortem which means after his death."

"I know what postmortem means, Special Agent Allen. I went to school."

"This could have been the work of anybody."

"Well, I may have a lead on that. We need to return to the precinct right away."

"A lead?"

"Kynami's wife."

David stood there skeptical. He knew dealing with a grieving widow especially a criminal's could cloud his judgement on the investigation. He had to prepare himself for what was about to come, but knew it wouldn't be enough.

"Captain Rodgers, I want an official report on my desk on this massacre by tomorrow morning."

"It'll be ready, Special Agent Allen." Captain Rodgers said showing David the door. David headed back with the Captain to the precinct to interview Kynami's widow.

## 16

## WHO?

Jacopo Saltinotti was standing in front of a mirror, admiring himself. An old man dressed in an elegant tailored suit was crouching next to him with a measuring tape into his hands, placed around Jacopo's thigh. Jacopo was getting fit for a white suit. He made slight turns left and right, inspecting every facet while studying its quality.

"Is it good, Signore?" the old man asked while adjusting his big glasses that made his eyes look like tennis balls.

"It needs a little work on the sleeves."

"I believe so, Signore. I'll fix it right away." the old man stood up heading to a small room in the back.

The bell hanging above the door rang, distracted Jacopo while he was checking himself out in the mirror. The man approached slowly as if he was avoiding to be spotted by Jacopo.

"Si?" Jacopo said without taking his eyes away from the mirror.

"Don Jacopo." the man voiced and Jacopo knew this messenger wasn't here to bring any good news. Jacopo remained silent, waiting for the man to kiss his hand and be given permission to speak.

"You may speak."

"We have word from the streets..."

Jacopo kept looking at his sleeves and the pants legs. "Maybe a little tighter in the legs, too?" he yelled to the old man, ignoring the messenger for a moment.

"The Jamaicans were wiped out. Kynami's dead and their entire stock of guns went missing."

"Who's behind this?"

"Our men asked around but nobody seems to know anything."

"But?"

"But we think it was Jessica Lombardi."

Jacopo clenched his fist to the sound of her name. He could feel his blood boiling. He took a short gasp, trying to calm himself.

"And why do we believe that?"

"The Italian families had a meeting the night before. They were probably planning this all along."

"When did we learn about that?" Jacopo asked almost playfully, with a soft smile. The man knew that smile well. Many have seen it hundreds of times and it was one of the worst signs of something bad to come from Jacopo.

"A few hours after the meeting, Don Jacopo." the man lowered his head out of shame and fear.

"And why weren't we informed about this meeting?"

"I don't know, sir."

"And I wasn't invited to the meeting?"

"No, Boss."

"Why do you think is that?"

"I think they are afraid of you."

"Do you really think so?"

"Si, Don Jacopo."

"Are we really sure that it was the Italians behind the attack?"

"It wasn't us. Nor the Triads or the Jews. Word is, the Task Force were planning to raid today, but missed the opportunity."

"Very well."

"I will leave, Don Jacopo?"

"You have one day to let me know if it was the Italians behind this."

The man stood there lost. He wasn't sure what to say. He watched Jacopo staring at his reflection in the mirror. Jacopo's eyes looked at him and the man felt as if an invisible hand had strangled him.

"Did I confuse you?"

"No, Don Jacopo. Right away."

"And learn who are they going to frame for the attack."

"Ok, Don Jacopo?"

"They will frame someone. Find out who and let me

know. That group will need my protection." Jacopo said adjusting the suit with serious face as the old man came back out of the room, carrying a little box with white threads, pins and brooches. The sound of the bell hanging above the door rang again as the old man saw Jacopo's messenger leave out.

"Problem with the men, Don Jacopo?"

"Nothing that can't be solved, Antonio."

"You're a man of your word."

"This pest - Jessica Lombardi - causes me concern."

"Why don't you take her of the picture?"

"That would send a bad message. It'll make my fear for her, nothing but evident. All the Italians will unite against me. I need to get rid of her soon and make it look like someone else did it."

"Polizia?"

"The police maybe."

"Si, Don Jacopo. Your suit is now fixed."

## 17

## THE GRIEVING WIDOW

David marched inside the police department, followed by Captain Rodgers. The department was nearly empty as most of the officers were at the scene of the last night's attack. David's footsteps echoed through the main hall as he walked towards the captain's office where Amelia Williams was with her child. There was one officer guarding the door.

The officer on duty saluted David as he walked inside. David had an attitude of a person whose office was his and took a seat in the captain's chair, sitting across from Amelia. The woman's face was buried behind a pile of Kleenex, visibly distraught.

David knew there was nothing he could say to comfort her and at best, he would gather few to no leads while she was in her current condition. It only helps if he tried. Last night's attack was a huge blow to his team and the city of New York.

"Mrs. Amelia Williams?"

"Yes?" the woman sobbed.

"My name is Special Agent David Allen. I'm here to ask you a few questions about your husband, Kynami 'Hatchet' Williams."

"He was a good man."

"I'm sure he was. Do you know what he did for a living?"

"He was a construction worker."

"How can a construction worker afford a two-story mansion in Kensington, Mrs. Williams? By the way, are you employed?"

"No, I'm not. My husband took out loans and we're struggling to pay it back."

"Mrs. Williams. I'm devastated to be the bearer of the bad news, but your husband wasn't just a construction worker."

"I know what you are going to say but it's not true."

"Mrs. Williams, your husband had been incarcerated. Am I correct?"

"I only know about the shoplifting incident. We needed milk for Anansi."

"Your son here, right?"

"Yes."

"Mrs. Williams, do you know why Kynami had the nickname 'Hatchet'? "

"I heard the tales and they're all lies. He was a good man."

"Kynami was been known to New York's law enforcement agencies for a long time. Your husband has his hands on all kinds of criminal activities including murder, racketeering, arsons and his final deed, gun smuggling."

Amelia remained silent. She felt poked in the chest by the David's words. Captain Rodgers had a serious look on his face.

"But you didn't know any of that, Mrs. Williams? Am I correct?"

"How could I? They're all lies made to slander my Kynami."

David started losing patience, but he believed the woman in front of him knew nothing about her husband's criminality. He grabbed a tissue and wiped the sweat off his face.

"Mrs. Williams. What was inside the box you received last night?"

Amelia let a long cry, beating her chest. The baby almost fell out of her arms. David stopped Rodgers from coming while he removed his jacket. He then got up and placed it on Mrs. Williams shoulders.

"I want to avenge the death of your husband, Mrs. Williams. I'm sure he was a good man and was killed unjustifiably. Can you help me?" David said sympathetically. Amelia nodded her head, taking another tissue that Captain Rodgers had now offered her.

"What was inside the box, Mrs. Williams?"

"My...my Kynami's head."

"What else?"

"A letter. For me."

"From whom?"

"It didn't have a name. The letter mentioned that I'm next if I make the same mistake as my husband."

"What mistake?"

"I don't know. He never did a bad thing in his life."

"Was there anything else in the letter?"

"Someone signed the letter: *'Kosher Nostra'*."

"Do you mean *Cosa Nostra*?"

"No, it said *Kosher Nostra*."

David turned his head looking at Captain Rodgers who was nodding in agreement with what was David thinking. "Thank you very much for your help, Mrs. Williams. We'll make sure that nothing happens to Anansi or you. Okay?"

"Okay," the woman sniffed.

"An officer will be in shortly to tell you about the Witness Protection Program. We want to make sure that you and your son's lives are protected."

"Thank you, Mr. Allen."

David got up and walked quickly to Captain Rodgers. "My office now, Captain." David whispered. Rodgers snorted and followed David.

Agent Allen took a seat behind his desk and opened the top drawer, searching for a file as the captain took a seat across him. A few moments later, David threw an open folder in front of the captain writing - Kosher Nostra Files.

The file was open to page three where the picture of a white man with black hair and big nose was pictured at the top right edge, held by a paper clip. "Alexander Lavie." David said tapping on the man's picture. "Are you familiar with this guy, Captain?"

"I was the one to put him behind bars a few years back. Of course, I am familiar with him."

"How could we miss this? It's the Jewish way of executing their rivals. The gift…"

"But they already shot the man dead."

"Yes. It doesn't add up but…"

"Why would the Jews want to move in on the Jamaicans? And why now?"

"That I don't know, Captain. It could be a set-up but we can't leave any stone uncovered."

"Agreed, Special Agent. How do you want us to proceed?"

"We'll make their lives a living hell. It doesn't matter how much time we spent hunting them down, we need to find Mister Alexander."

"Special Agent Allen, even if we find him, we have no solid proof of his involvement directly with Kosher Nostra."

"I know, Captain. I just want to rattle Kosher Nostra's nests a little, so they know they're not welcome in this town no more."

"If we take out Lavie, I believe that the rest of them will think twice about setting up here again. Just think about the Domino effect."

"I hope so. But I don't think Kosher Nostra has nothing to do with Kynami's murder. Someone's messing with our heads and I think it might be the Italians." David pointed at Jacopo's folder sitting on his desk which was thinner than the others. "They're plotting on something. I just have a weird feeling about this."

"Maybe but the Italians aren't stupid enough to leave a note in a box with a head? What about the Chinese?"

"The Triads? They have gone underground since they bribed half of the precincts in New York to run their illegal petty shops."

"Davi-"

"Special Agent Allen."

"Special Agent Allen, the Triads do not own any of our officers."

"Not today, Captain. Place a BOLO on Mister Lavie and let's see how this plays out."

The captain nodded and left out of the room without saying another word. David stood in front of the open files, trying to figure out who was behind this. He believed Jacopo may had something to do with it, but he had to put up a smokescreen to not give away any leads on the investigation. David couldn't trust a single person inside the precinct, not even his own Captain. The facts were the only pieces he could trust.

**18**

---

## RISE OF AN EMPIRE

For the next few months, after Kynami's death, Jessica took over all the territories the Jamaicans controlled, gaining more ground for her Italian syndicate. Sabina took control over the gun smuggling business as the assets were being laundered through the churches of the Episcopo family.

Andrea bought out a good number of police officers making the lives of rival families such as the Salinottis harder. They were instructed to look the other way when they noticed something suspicious that involving their new partners.

In the meantime, the NYPD, CIA, and FBI had turned all of its attention to the Kosher Nostra, the Jewish-American organized crime suspected off killing the Jamaicans. The drug businesses and prostitution went down as more police raids were conducted against the Jews. They were scrutinized to the point that the officers that pulled them over, yanked off their kippahs believing that they were stashing drugs underneath them.

As Kosher Nostra was getting ripped apart piece by piece, Jessica slowly, with precision like a professional chess player, got into the drug business. The demand was getting higher while the supply was low. It didn't take long before Kosher Nostra began running out of money and Alexander Lavie, who was their main endorser, was forced to sell a majority of his shares to smaller clients who were out of the police's crosshairs.

Unknowingly, Alexander Lavie had sold most of his business shares to Jessica Lombardi, as most of the independent shareholders were actually working for her. Alexander collected few dollars, but Jessica was the principal owner. The CIA kept pushing with more raids to Alexander's hideouts, forcing him to continually change locations. The profits he received from his shares were not enough to sustain him or his business.

Alexander devastated, sat in a small coffee store with two of his cousins. The men were standing a few tables away, keeping an eye on the once-proud leader of the Lavie family. Alexander looked over today's newspaper, inspecting the front-page's picture. Most of his hideouts were placed on twenty-four-hour watch by the OC Task Force after being raided. *"The Jewish Criminal is still at large"* the first-page headline read. They couldn't prove he was involved in Kosher Nostra, but law enforcement had found enough damning evidence in his safe houses to put away for life.

Alexander sighed grabbing his cup; his hand was shaking, unable to keep it still. He took a sip and kept reading the article. The people of New York and the media were crucifying him. Alexander looked up at his father's store; a store which was passed down for three generations. It was one of his last surviving business ventures.

The coffee shop was empty. The waitress was idly looking out of the window, with the look of a person begging for her shift to end. Alexander shifted his attention back to the newspaper when he heard the door open. Before he could open his mouth and order his men, unknown men already had guns drawn.

Five men had masks on their faces, carrying Thompsons. Alexander reached for his gun inside his suit jacket, but a female voice told *"There is no need, Alexander."* It was Jessica Lombardi taking a seat across from him, taking off her raincoat and purple scarf.

"Have we met?" the man asked with an eastern accent as he was still trying to reach for his gun.

"Not in person. We haven't."

"Who are you?"

"My name is Jessica Lombardi." Jessica said smiling and waving her hair in front of him.

"Italian? Do you work with the Saltinottis? Tell Jacopo what I told him last time. They will bury me in the ground before I accept his protection."

Jessica leaned on the wooden table and stared the worried man in the eyes.

"I'm no Saltinotti, Signore Alexander Lavie. On the contrary."

"The Italians used to run this city. Not anymore."

"I disagree. I run this city for now on."

"Look what's going on around you, woman. The Jamaicans are gone and my businesses are failing."

"I am the one behind the Jamaicans' fall."

"What?"

"You heard me. And I'm the reason half of your business ventures are mines now."

"You fucking bitch!" the man shouted trying to reach for his gun, but the consecutive clicks of men's' guns made him think twice. Lavie then placed his hands in front of him.

"Please."

"I'm not here to kill you, Mr. Lavie. You saw what happened to Kynami. If I wanted you dead, you would have already been."

"What do you want?"

"A business partner." Jessica chuckled waving at the waitress hiding behind the counter, peaking. "Black coffee, please" Jessica said charmingly before staring back at Alexander.

"You're a new player in the business. Why do you want me?"

"I want someone to run it. Someone who knows how."

"The NYPD is up my ass. I can't help." Alexander scoffed leaning back in his leather seat as the waiter brought coffee with trembling hands. The waiter put down the coffee and ran behind the counter, turning her eyes away from the men with guns.

"Let me worry about that. I'll give them something more important to deal with."

"What do you want?"

"Forty percent."

"That's fucking crazy!"

"Then, I think we're done here today. Have a nice day, Mister Lavie." Jessica took a sip and stood up as her men pointed their guns to Alexander and his two bodyguards. She couldn't hold back the smile on her face as she put on her raincoat. One of her men opened the restaurant's door for her.

Alexander slammed his fist on the table, causing his coffee to spill over like a brown river. "Wait." he said pleading holding his hands in the air. Jessica paused without turning around. "Okay. I am in. But I need protection and in God's name…no NYPD or Feds."

"Do we have a deal then?"

"Yes, No NYPD, no Feds."

"Let me handle your troubles, Mr. Alexander. I'll make the arrangements. Thank you for your business."

Jessica said playfully before heading out to the dark street, followed by her bodyguards. They drove her to a playground near the beach where Alberto was taking pictures of Luca, holding an ice cream cone with two scoops of strawberry.

Jessica approached them smiling and went to pat little

Luca's head. "May I join?" she asked merrily. "Are you done with the business?" Alberto asked. Jessica nodded and posed next to Luca as Alberto took a picture of the two.

Meanwhile back in the coffee shop, Alexander remained speechless, unable to fathom what had just happened. This Italian woman just came inside his establishment and took over his businesses. Deep down, Alexander knew he was in some deep shit. What choice did he have unless he wanted his life back even if it meant working for the Italians?

19

## LET'S CELEBRATE

Jessica was back at her father's desk, the place where she had organized and executed the perfect plan to make New York underworld bow to her commands. There were a pile of files on the corner of her desk of the day-to-day operations. Everything she pulled off in the past few months was jotted down in those files.

Jessica put out her cigarette and looked at the ashtray, filled with buds and ashes. She knew smoking was bad, but it was the only thing that kept her mind focused.

The silence inside her office was a blessing. They were the best moments she enjoyed throughout the day. Jessica finally smiled, now able to concentrate. Then a soft knock on the door disrupted her enjoyable silence. "Come in." she said taking another drag as she turned on the desk lamp.

Andrea walked inside, followed by the heads of the

Italian families. Each walked inside taking seats on the leather chairs circling Jessica's desk. Everyone had a smile on their face and Julius raised his arm, displaying a bottle of Barolo, the finest red wine from Italy. "What's this for?" Jessica asked.

"We wanted to show our appreciation, Donna." Andrea said placing wine glasses in front of everyone.

"Can't this wait? We have a very important meeting." Jessica said as a glass was placed in front of her. Julius opened the bottle and poured. "A little celebration first wouldn't delay our meeting." Julius said as he poured.

Sabina raised her glass first. "To our leader, our Donna." she said and everyone raised their wine glasses. "Without you Jessica, Jacopo would probably had black-mailed us." She continued taking the first sip. "To Jessica" the rest whispered and drank. Jessica felt awkward but went along with the festivities.

Respect from the heads of the Italians would only bring her joy. She made it but there were still loose ends to tie up. "So, let's get down to business." She interrupted putting her glass down on the desk.

"Sabina, how are the guns?"

"With the Jamaicans out of the picture and the police dealing with Kosher Nostra, it couldn't have been better."

"Glad to hear. Our men?"

"Armed to the teeth with the latest. I contacted the suppliers and more weapons are coming in as early as tomorrow. We're expecting a large shipment."

"I'm glad, Sabina. It seems like you have everything under control. How about our finances, Paolo?"

"We've invested in a few more churches and community outreach groups for the poor to keep funneling the money through." Paolo chuckled followed by laughter from the rest in the room. "Everything is under control. Keep it coming and we know how to make the neighborhoods look good." He reassured Jessica.

"Excellent. And you, Andrea?"

"We have three precincts; all the cops the Jamaicans and Kosher Nostra had on their payrolls now are on ours. The streets are quieter with the Task Force off our backs."

"Since everything's in order and the books align with what you all told me, it's time for the next phase of our plan."

"Is this necessary?" Andrea asked with concern.

"What do you mean, Andrea?" Jessica raised her eyebrows waiting his reply.

"We have a good amount of cash coming in. We control the police, the guns, the City. Let's no get greedy."

Jessica put out her cigarette and lit another one. The room became silent as Jessica took a long drag. Andrea fixed his tie and waited for her response.

"Andrea…" Jessica started choosing her words carefully. "We're not petty criminals or a street gang. I told you before we began this operation. I'm not doing this for money or power. I want New York to bleed. I want to make the police force to bleed. I want that *bastardo* Jacopo to crawl begging for his life back. And hell, I want New York to bow to our command. Do you think we are anywhere close to this yet, Andrea?" Jessica's words came out like a string of gunshots aimed at Andrea. Every member of the group was mute.

Andrea kept fixing his tie, nervous. He didn't want Jessica to see him as a traitor nor the rest of the family heads. The power of the Lombardi name since the day he sided with the families couldn't be matched.

"No, we are not, Donna Jessica."

"Good. Don't think like this ever again, Andrea. There is never enough."

"I'm sorry, Donna Jessica." he stood up kissing Jessica's hand.

"As I was saying, Sofia and Julius have an excellent plan that will go into effect as of this moment." Jessica said pointing towards Julius who nodded. "Alexander Lavie, the lead financier of Kosher Nostra is now working for us."

"What the fuck?" Sabina shouted almost dropping her glass down to floor. "We do not work with other gangs, my lady."

Sofia came inside the office and stood in the back. "Luca's asleep, Sabina."

Sabina turned around and her face turned gloomier.

"Please let Jessica explain. I'm sorry for the trouble, I have caused you in the past. Please forgive me." Sofia said smiling.

"Ok, Sofia. I forgive you. Thank you."

"Alexander Lavie, as of today is working for us. He gracefully handed half of his businesses over and agreed to run it for us as long as we keep the police off his back." Jessica continued.

"How are we going to do this?"

"This is where you come in, Andrea. I want our police informants to mislead the investigation and divert the probe on the Triads."

"This will not work for long, Donna Jessica."

"It will work long enough for us to take down the Triads, the same way we took down the Jamaicans."

"The Jamaicans were just gun runners. The Triads control as much as we do. Plus they have more manpower.."

"I know. So, we will carry out a precise takeover. I want you to find out who their leader is and send the OC Task Force after him."

"It's a crazy move."

"A crazy one that if it succeeds, the cops won't be able to stop us."

"Will they fall for the bait?"

"They will. The Task Force will not ignore a lead from the second in command."

Silence covered the room as the families were evaluating their options. Andrea seemed skeptical. "Fine." he said. "I'll take care of it…tonight." he said as if he had another option. Jessica was merely giving him the semblance of free will. He trusted Jessica's judgement. So far, all her moves have proven successful. There was no reason to doubt her now.

"As of tomorrow, we take another giant step in the direction of what we are building." Jessica said getting up extending her hands. "We achieved so much in such little time. Just a few more loose ends tied up and New York will be ours."

The family leaders stood up cheering and clapping, following their leader's example.

"I'll be in touch." she said showing them the door as they got up leaving the room, one by one. Sofia headed outside to escort them to the front door.

Jessica sat, lighting another cigarette thinking the plan would be a success. It would be another step closer in making her father and Francesco proud. At that moment, Jessica realized that she was building something for her son, Luca's future.

**20**

———

## THE FAVOR

Agent Toney Miles drove up his driveway after looking through his rearview mirror, sighting a patrol car circling his neighborhood. For the past few months, Miles grew paranoid for his life and his family's.

His wife and son called him twice a day. He called them more than that making sure his family was safe. Even though he hasn't heard from Andrea since the first ordeal, he knew the Italians would come knocking on his door again. Miles only hoped that he didn't have to murder anyone for the sake of his family.

Miles pressed the code unlocking the door and entered. It's been a long day. The nonstop raids on Kosher Nostra weren't boosting his morale. The Task Force had emptied over twenty warehouses and arrested over a hundred men; all suspected to be working for Lavie.

His boss, Special Agent David Allen was pushing him to his limit. Tony believed David made this his personal vendetta. He shared little to no information with Tony or Captain Rodgers. There was no way Miles could offer the Italians any information because he had none.

Miles took off his shoes and went to deactivate the second alarm system. It was turned off and Miles knew the deal. He wanted to get this over with and walked to the kitchen where three armed men and Andrea were there waiting. Andrea was enjoying himself a cup of tea as if he was the rightful owner of the house.

"Bonasera, Agent Miles." Andrea said sipping slowly. Miles pulled a chair across Andrea and took a seat.

"Let's get straight to the point. What is it now?"

"Ha! straight to the point, Agent?"

The men and Andrea chuckled.

"What do you want?"

"A favor."

"I know that."

"A smaller one this time."

"Just get to the point."

"I want you to mislead the Task Force's investigation."

"What does that even mean?"

"I want you to stop the raids against Kosher Nostra."

"Why would I do that?"

"You know why, Agent Miles. Per la tua famiglia"

"How? David is in command."

"David?"

"Agent David Allen. He doesn't trust a single soul in our department."

"I bet."

"Just tell me what you want me to do."

"We want you to go after the Triads."

"David knows the Triads have nothing to do with this."

"Even after you show him this?" Andrea pushed a folder towards Miles. "Have a look," he said taking another sip.

Miles opened the file. "Are the Triads trying to take over Alexander's territory?"

"No, but that's what you will present to Agent Allen."

"He will never fall for it."

"He's too determined to let it any piece of evidence go uncounted."

Miles knew deep down inside that Andrea was right. These Italians are pressing the right buttons at the right moment. When the raids start becoming pointless, David would go for the bigger fish and work his way down.

"What do you get out of all this?"

"We'll be free to hire Alexander ourselves."

"What if I refuse?"

"Maybe you should check out the new set of photos of your wife and son at Disneyland. You already get my drift."

Miles felt bad. The Italians weren't bluffing. They were following his family's every step. The system that swore to serve and protect him couldn't stop these criminals.

"Okay. Give me until tomorrow evening."

"We shall. Prepare to tell Mr. David that you received an anonymous tip from one of your informants."

"He won't believe me."

"The worst thing that can happen is that you get dropped from the investigation."

"That would end my career."

"Maybe. But this is more important than you think."

"Tomorrow."

"One more thing. Who's running the Triads?"

"How come you don't know?"

"Let's say that getting to Agent Miles has caused some paranoia around the department."

"Mr. Zhang. If that's his real name."

"Thank you for your help, once again, Agent Miles. We'll be in touch. Consider your debt paid for now."

"I'm off the leash?"

"For now. But if I hear you fooling around in my business, I'll be paying a personal visit to Disneyland to say hi to your family."

Miles groaned and slammed the file on the table. "God damn, you!"

"You'll thank me later. Get some rest, Agent. Tomorrow, you have a big day ahead of you." Andrea said taking the cup of tea with him.

## 21

## WHAT ABOUT THE TRIADS?

David was sitting at his desk, bouncing from one file to the next. His office was cluttered with dozens of files on the desk and laid out across the floor. Over the past few months, he became obsessed with Kosher Nostra. David also suspected there was a new power player was waiting in the lurches to rise up. Jacopo was up to something, but David could only lean on the facts of his investigation and right now all the evidence was pointing to the Jews.

The evidence obtained from all Kosher Nostra hideouts didn't lead to any connections between the Jamaicans, Triads or the Italians. He ordered his detectives to keep digging and searching for anything that could stick but many of the informants and CIs on the streets were on the mob's payroll.

David Allen spent years solving hundreds of organized crime cases including Joe Colombo's associates.

Still, he felt like his was drowning in his own swimming pool. When frustrated, David knocked the files off his desk and cleared his drawers out to restart. David's boss back at the FBI even started doubting his ability to solve the city's organized crime woes.

The dark bags under his eyes and unkept hair started giving him the look of a madman possessed. *How did you do it, Miller? You were unorthodox, sloppy and blinded. But you still won that damn medal. I read your file. You were an embarrassment to the FBI and still, you managed to take down the most notorious families in New York.*

David spoke to himself regularly reminding him of the task at hand. This morning he had forgotten what day it was. His perfect routine was being affected by one unsolvable case. David's thoughts kept spiraling into circles of crazy theories until he heard a knock on his door.

The person that knocked didn't wait for an answer and came right inside.

"Agent Miles. This isn't a good time."

"I believe it is, sir." Miles said waving the file that Andrea handed him last evening. Agent Miles spent the last few months struggling to keep a good face around the office. Underneath, he was basically flipped into a professional liar.

"What is this, Miles?" David said rubbing his red eyes, trying to find a second of comfort.

"The Triads, sir. It was them all along."

David looked up at Miles with disbelief. "What the hell is this?"

"You heard me. It was Triads behind all the attack on the Jamaicans," said Agent Miles throwing the folder in front of David.

David took the file but his hands were trembling due to the lack of sleep. He opened it, reading it for about a minute.

"Miles. Where did you get this?"

"An informant, sir."

"Miles, don't make me ask you again. Where the fuck did you get this information?"

"It was left on my doorsteps by one of my reliable informants, sir."

"Agent Miles. None of this makes any sense. The Triads have nothing to do with gun smuggling or the drug business."

"Look at the numbers, sir. Everything adds up."

"These numbers seem botched down to the core. Half of these estates and businesses aren't even controlled by the Triads."

"Sir…"

"Agent Miles. Do you see this department's current situation? I don't want to keep getting pushed around by these elephants in the room. They wanted you to hand me this. Who would want to take out the Triads? The Jamaicans? The Bloods? The Crips? The Albanian Boys? Who the fuck—?

"Sir…"

"Let me finish! Or has Alexander Lavie pulled a Houdini on us? Gone from the face of the Earth!"

"Alexander Lavie was seen yesterday, sir. He made a deal with a mysterious buyer. An Italian."

"What? Why didn't we investigate that?"

"The information just came by one of our CIs a few hours ago. A witness from one of our old criminal cases had recognized him."

"What if Alexander is playing us?"

"Sir, with all due respect. You look terrible. Your judgment seems clouded. What if this evidence is solid? What if we can nail the Triads finally?"

"And then Alexander's arrest would just be a joke." David said to himself drawn back in his thoughts. "If the Triads were out of the picture, his Task Force could focus their full attention on Lavie who was already bleeding to death." David mumbled to himself.

"Thank you, Agent Miles. Good work. This case is getting on my fucking nerves."

"I know sir. It's getting to me, too."

"Take the rest of the day off, Toney. I'll keep you posted if I have some questions."

"There's no need to do everything by yourself, Special Agent. We know where this will lead."

"Please don't. Not now."

Agent Miles left the office leaving David alone. The veteran police officer just earned his family a few more days. At this point, Tony didn't even feel bad for what he had done. David's Task Force were hunting down criminal gangs like they were supposed to but just off a bit. Miles could live with that.

David kept reading the file from front to back when he got back in his office. The information inside just didn't make sense but if any of it were true, he would be the agent that nailed the Triads. Possibly, causing a domino effect on the rest. David grinned knowing it has been days since he made progress. Maybe it was time to start a war with the Triads.

## 22

## REBIRTH

The days that followed were the worst for the Triads' in the history of New York. The Organized Task Force under the lead of David Allen now focused all of their attention on the Triads as the first few pieces of evidence pointed to the Asian gang taking over the drug trade. That gave David enough leverage to continue raiding ignoring most of the details in that file he was given by Miles.

Under the radar of law enforcement, the renown leader of Kosher Nostra, Alexander Lavie was up and running again. His drug business was flourishing while Jessica controlled almost half of New York's police force and most of Lavie's profits. Her empire was rising faster than anyone could expect. David was doing all the work for her. He was too busy with his task of shutting down the Triads he couldn't stop to think clearly.

Paranoid as he was, his associates never had a saying in his task force objectives. The CIA, FBI, and Mayor were pleased with just getting results. Criminals were put behind bars and David was a step closer to shutting down the Triads completely. However, in the territories his raids left behind, Jessica marched in and seized what was left, rebuilding, with no one to stop her. No one suspected Jessica was becoming the biggest threat to New York City except for one man.

Jacopo Saltinotti strolled through the crowded market of Chinatown. Cleaning his teeth with a toothpick, he stopped to stare at full moon that was decorating the night. Pushing through the crowd, Jacopo ignored the constant shouting of street vendors trying to get people to buy.

He took a sharp right turn down a dark dirty alleyway. His footsteps crunched as he walked on broken glass, reaching a rusty iron door with the following written in Chinese: 草药 (Herbs). Jacopo banged on the door three times, waiting for ten seconds and then banged again. A small slider opened and a man's eyes stared at him as the music from inside could be heard loudly.

"Name?"

"Jacopo Saltinotti."

The man closed the slide unlocking the door. Jacopo was met with golden orange lights of candles on both sides of the entrance. He passed through seeing some beautiful women lined up against a wall. The smell of whiskey and cigars scented the next room packed with men shouting at one another. They were leaning over a table padded with green velcro throwing dice and playing cards. "Follow me," the man said walking between the tables, heading to the back of the room.

Jacopo followed the man and after a few seconds, he was at Mr. Zhang's office. The office looked worse than the factory, lending to the purpose of running his illegal gambling operation and nothing more. "Take a seat Jacopo." Mr. Zhang said taking a sip from his tea cup. "May I offer you some tea?" he asked.

"No, Signore Zhang. I'm here for business only."

"Business? Haha! I thought you wanted some of my ladies' services in the front. What business do we have that you are referring to, Mr. Jacopo?" Zhang mocked with his men standing behind him laughing, holding their guns.

"Haha! Really funny!?"

"Ok, seriously. You said you'd offer me protection and where is it now?"

"Don't lose your faith so easily, Mr. Zhang."

"My organization's being torn apart by the hour."

"I'm well aware."

"I've been paying you all this time and what for?"

"Have you have any troubles before?"

"No. But…"

"Well, then. Now that the Organized Crime Task Force are involved, it'll require a little something extra."

"I don't think I made myself clear, Mr. Jacopo."

"I think you did."

The men behind him pointed their guns at Jacopo.

"Any last words, Jacopo Saltinotti?"

"Yes, Zhang." Jacopo said taking a seat.

"Speak."

"I will make the Task Force problem go away by tomorrow night."

"And how would you do that, Jacopo?"

"That's none of your concern, Mr. Zhang,"

"And why didn't you do that already?"

"It requires some extra reinforcements. And the price is up to forty-five percent."

"You're fucking joking!"

"I'm not. Kill me and my Italians friends will kill you and your operation before you exit this shithole."

Zhang signaled for his men to lower their guns. He knew Jacopo was right.

"My men are on standby and if I don't return in five minutes, they'll consider me dead and will move in. How do you want to do this?" Jacopo looked at him sinisterly.

"Okay, okay. Tomorrow night. Not a single day longer. Otherwise, you're done, Jacopo." Zhang threatened trying to regain control, but they both knew Jacopo had the upper hand.

"Expect my call."

"No call. Come in person."

"You have nothing to worry about Zhang. Tomorrow, your problems will cease."

Jacopo got up and headed out. A few minutes afterward, he was strolling through Chinatown, walking with his hands behind his back. He looked up at the sky fondling with his toothpick. Without knowing, Jessica had handed him the best gift ever. It was time for the Saltinottis to get in on the action.

## 23

## FAMILY HONOR

Jessica sat beside her father at his hospital bed. The constant rhythmic beeping of the heart monitor gave her faith. She tried shutting her eyes, blocking the tears from pouring down; tears of sadness and joy at the same time. The doctors informed her that his medical condition had grown worse by the day and said only a miracle could bring him out of his coma. Jessica pushed away the bad speculations, grabbing her father's hand and squeezing it tightly for warmth.

"Hey, Papà." Jessica sniffled as her tears found their way down her cheeks. "We're back on top," she said smiling.

"Since the day I came back, I've made New York pay, Papà. For what they did to you, to us, to our family. I'm sure you're proud wherever you are," Jessica paused taking a short breath. "If you could, you would probably denounce me but I did it. I proved you wrong. I am capable of running not just one family, Papà. I'm running all of them except for the Saltinottis Stronzos. I'm within a few feet of the finish line and I just wanted you to let you know you were wrong about your daughter." Jessica cried as tears overcame her.

"You thought I couldn't succeed but here I am. The proud Lombardi. Michael's bambina! Your bambina is running New York, Papà. How do you feel now? You must feel like a fool right? Not trusting me. Criticizing me all the time when I screwed up." Jessica lashed out at Michael as if he was the one to blame for all the screwups she had since arriving from Italy. All those things she couldn't tell him in person were bottled up inside her.

"But Giovanni was the prodigy. Giovanni would run the family. Guess what? He's in jail and I am running the whole damn operation now!" Jessica said under her breath. At that moment, Jessica placed her face inside her father's arms. She cried like a little girl.

"I'm sorry, Papà. I can't bear the sight of seeing you like this anymore. Oh, you, Giovanni, Francesco and Luca would be so proud. I know so." She paused looking at his motionless body. "I just wanted to hear a congratulation. A well done, Jessica. Something?"

I'll make our family proud again, Papà. I promise. I promised Grandma Serena and Francesco. To you. I promise, I will never let you down again." Jessica stood up wiping her tears from her face. "I love you Papà."

Sofia entered the room and rushed towards Jessica, giving her a warm hug, clutching her in her arms. "Are you okay, Jessica? I just got your message."

"What did you hear?"

"Enough to know you needed a hug."

"I don't know what has come over me."

"Love, loss, fear of losing him. Of letting go."

"It's hard, isn't it?"

"It is. But it's part of life." Hiding her pain, Jessica could see Sofia was putting on a strong face for her which gave her comfort. She was the one who buried her husband and both of her children only months apart. Sofia was the strongest woman Jessica ever knew.

"Thank you, Sofia."

"I'm always here for you, Jessica. We're in this together. You're my daughter." Sofia smiled as they both laughed; a laugh that turned into a nervous emotional roar they couldn't contain. They kept embracing each other and then proceeded to sit beside the bedside of Michael Lombardi.

"So, why did you need me to come here?"

"I'm pulling the plug, Sofia."

"What? Why?"

"The doctors say he has no chance of surviving."

"There's still time."

"He's suffering, Sofia. This is no life for a Don."

"He's sleeping well, Jessica. Don't let go of the only person in your family you revere."

"I have to move on. It's time. I've made peace with myself."

Both women waited silently. Jessica kept staring at the heart monitor while Sofia had her eyes fixed on Michael, worried for Jessica. "Do you think this is the right thing to do?"

"I believe it is. We need to move forward. My father would want this."

"He loved you so much, Jessica. The man will be respected forever amongst us. *Riposa in pace, Don Michael!*"

"Thank you. Can you call in the doctors?"

"Okay."

Sofia left out the room while Jessica remained there staring at her father. Every time she saw his white pale skin and half-opened soulless eyes, she felt bad for him. She grabbed his hand and rubbed it. "I guess this is goodbye then Papà. I'm sorry for all the trouble I've caused you in this world. I'll make you proud. *In nomine patris et filli et spiritus sanctus. Riposa in pace, Amen.*" Jessica said, making the sign of the cross as a tear came down her eye; the last tear left inside her.

Jessica got up and stepped out of the room as the doctors came back with Sofia. A male doctor grabbed Jessica by the shoulder and looked her in her red eyes. "Are you sure, Miss. Lombardi?" he asked. "Yes." Jessica said trembling. "I'm sorry for your loss. When you are ready, please sign here," the doctor said handing her a form. Jessica looked it while her hands began shaking.

Her right one stalled above the signature line. She hesitated and closed her eyes shut.

Sofia put her arm around Jessica's shoulder. Jessica looked at Sofia and signed the form. She handed it to the doctor and immediately ran down the hallway. She wanted to be as far away as possible and never wanted to return to the hospital again.

## 24

## BETRAYAL

The repetitive beeps of the alarm clock echoed in the room as David slowly opened his eyes. They felt sore and dry. David rubbed them and got up off the card boxes he had been sleeping on for the short part of the night. It was a night spent inside the police station's archive room, studying cases and just about anything on the Triads, Italians, Kosher Nostra, the Jamaican Posse and the other criminal gangs in his jurisdiction.

Just yesterday, he received an anonymous tip about Jessica, daughter of the infamous Michael Lombardi. He was briefed that the notorious leader's daughter had popped up in town using an alias. Miss. Lombardi came to America from Italy by boat. The authorities didn't even think about tracing her whereabouts after being interrogated by Agent Garcia. David had no evidence on her involvement in the city's organized crime, but she could be a big piece missing in the puzzle. He wanted to find out what was the motives behind the war that ravaged New York in the last few months and did it have anything to do with her arrival.

David moved around like a doctor working doubles at a hospital. He buttoned up his open shirt and tried fixing his tie, but after a few seconds of struggling, he gave up. He headed towards the room's exit feeling hungry. Once David got back to his office, he gathered the remainder of his notes on the investigation; an investigation that became endless as the days went by.

The precinct was empty on Sunday morning. No clerks, bail bondsmen or maintenance staff were around. The few officers on duty that morning were out in the streets, arresting suspected Triads and raiding their safe-houses, one after the other, like a wild witch-hunt. David proved to be an exemplary agent and his work was impeccable. But he couldn't shake off the feeling that his job performance was breeding results. He felt like a pawn in a shit load of NYPD bureaucracy. His agency was tracing suspected bank accounts and assets faster than anyone in the state of New York, but law enforcement's efforts weren't bringing any new leads. Not the real ones he wished for.

Flopping into his leather chair, David compared last night's evidence with the FBI's data. Some things added up, but if Jessica Lombardi was behind this, she was doing an excellent job at staying out of the spotlight. Unlike the other criminal networks at least.

The sound of David's pen writing furiously disrupted the normal silence of his office. He kept writing with such a bored look on his face. His once calligraphic letters were now a bunch of incomprehensible scribbles. A ten-year-old would have done a better job at keeping notes than him right now.

During the next hour, David began to realize his writing made no sense. He was bouncing around from one subject to the next, mixing up the notes. Out of frustration, he squeezed his pen almost making it explode and grabbed his notes and threw them against the wall, making them land on top of the hundreds of papers that were already there.

David grabbed his forehead, breathing heavily like a runner after a marathon.

Then someone knocked on the door. After staring at for fifteen seconds, David yelled "Come in," trying making his desk presentable. Captain Rodgers came inside quickly with something on his mind.

"David."

"Special Agent Allen, Captain. How many times——"

"We don't have time for that kind formality bullshit, Mr. Allen. A new clue in the case just came in."

"Captain, with all due respect. This is the third time I

heard this shit this month. I don't have time for jigsaw puzzles."

"Well, you'll have time for this one. We believe that it pieces everything together."

"What is it, then?"

"I need you to come with me right away. It's not safe to talk inside the station."

David finally had a glimpse of hope. Captain Rodgers looked worried as there was something behind his compelling tone. "Why so, Captain?" David wrote something on a piece of paper. Is this office breached?

Rodgers rushed to front of his desk, taking a seat, grabbing the same piece of paper and wrote "Affirmative."

David eyes lit up. If the precinct was breached, then who else has been compromised in David's investigation. That's what he needed to know; *quick answers.*

Without saying another word, the two men walked to an empty ward, heading to a rarely used elevator. Captain Rodgers pressed the top floor's button and the elevator shaft moved upwards, heading to the roof. David try to speak but Rodgers raised his finger, silencing him.

Since the first day he worked out of this precinct, it was the first time he saw Rodgers like this. A few moments later, the elevator doors opened and the two were in front of a rusty staircase, ready to collapse if someone stepped on it. Captain Rodgers without speaking climbed it and opened another door at its end, revealing sunlight from outside.

David followed as a strong wind grazed his face from outside. Rodgers was standing on the rooftop with the same disturbed look.

Captain Rodgers made a gesture with his hands, urging David to come forward. David walked out cautiously, placing his hand on holster. "What's this about, Captain Rodgers?"

"I found out who the mole is David."

"What mo-" David interrupted. He was caught off-guard, knowing that he hasn't shared details with anyone from his strike team since that one incident with Agent Miles "Who is it?"

"You are not the only one doing actual police work around here, David."

"Who the fuck is it, Captain?"

"As being Captain of this precinct, I have been instructed to give a press conference on the matter later today. Chief Deputy Arthur Jones is on his way to the Precinct to brief us on its contents."

"From Internal Affairs?"

"Yes. Believe me, David. Once you know the name of the officer who compromised our investigation, it will clear up many questions we may have."

"Where's he now?"

"Arthur should be here in a matter of———." Rodgers was interrupted.

The roof door flew opened and a man with a loose tie and a creased shirt joined the two men. His thick blond hair was waving as the wind passed. He adjusted his thick-bifocals, grabbing his briefcase tightly against his body.

"Captain."

"Arthur."

"Special Agent David Allen. What a pleasure!"

"The pleasure's mine, Deputy Chief Jones." David said worried. This situation was getting stickier by the moment.

"Deputy Chief Jones, you instructed me to give press conference on our mole later today. Are we still all clear?"

"Yes, Captain Rodgers. It's a go." Deputy Chief Jones then pulled out a small tape recorder from his briefcase.

Agent Allen then asked, "Are you sure we should be doing this right here?"

"Since this precinct has been compromised, I don't want to take any chances in case any of us go missing." Arthur said as he pressed the tape recorder's play button, nodding to David to come closer. *"This is Arthur Jones, Head of the Internal Affairs Division. Badge number 1317. Captain Timothy Rogers of the Seventh District Police Department of the State of New York, Badge number 7391 who will give an official statement in the presence of..."* Arthur paused and nodded to David to speak.

*"Special Agent David Allen. Head of the Organized Crime Task Force under the FBI and CIA, Badge number 20198"* David said as Arthur moved the microphone closer to Rodgers. "It's all yours, Captain."

Rodgers cleared his throat searching to find the right words before speaking.

*"Colleagues at Internal Affairs, over the last few months, an inside team of special investigators apart from the OC Task Force have followed leads that has pointed to the organized investigation headed by Special Agent David Allen have been misled on pretenses headed by one individual inside our police department. Agent Tony Miles, of the NYPD, second-in-command of the Organized Crime Task Force obscured the team's investigation misleading Special Agent Allen into an endless witch-hunt."* The Captain paused taking a short breath, trying to form his next sentence.

David's eyes widened in shock as a series of flashbacks dawned on him. The folder that magically dropped at Miles's doorstep, his illness and random call-outs. Everything was lining up. David was hooked to Rodger's words like a fish out of the water.

*"We believe that Agent Tony Miles was not working alone. We are still in the process of uncovering the root of his corrupt police work. Tony Miles will be formally charged at the end of today's press conference."* Captain Rodgers looked at Jones weirdly as he turned off the recorder.

Deputy Jones took a step back, realizing something was wrong. David was caught in the suspense of the moment. Rodgers grabbed for David's gun and pulled the trigger. Two loud bangs echoed and Arthur was lying on the ground, dying. "David. Don't move!" Rodgers whispered grabbing the recorder.

David stood there mesmerized. "Why Captain?" David pleaded as Rodgers pointed his gun at him.

"I'm sorry, David. I had no other choice."

"What did they offer you? Money?"

"I have a daughter, David. Just like Miles. I can't blame the man."

"We can protect you and your family."

"You're stupid, David. At least, Agent Miller knew the system was corrupt."

"The man got a medal for a massacre."

"The man actually did good work, David!"

"How long? How long are you working for them?"

"Since the Bloodshed."

"The Lombardis? The Guilanis? The Jews?"

"No."

The roof top door opened again and two men, dressed as painters, came carrying a blue tarp. They moved the body of Deputy Jones with ease, wrapping it with the tarp. Behind the two men, a man appeared in a white suit. His face was hidden under a white cap with a red line decorating it.

The man removed it theatrically and performed a bow to Rodgers and then to David. "Buongiorno, Agent Allen." the man said walking next to Captain Rodgers. "Excellent work."

"Really Captain Rodgers? Working for this piece of shit, Jacopo Saltinotti?"

"Be careful what you say, Mr. Allen. I would tread lightly."

"No. Let him speak. Do you have something to say, Special Agent?"

"You're going fucking down, Jacopo."

"From where I am standing, I'm actually going up, Signore Davide. It looks like you'll be going down unless you do as I say from now on."

David remained silent. He couldn't believe what had just happened.

"I have your gun, your prints and the Captain's statement. Oh, and a dead body." Jacopo said while grabbing the gun with a latex glove and placing it inside an evidence bag, along with the tape recorder.

David sighed; the moan of anger and betrayal. But most of all, he felt like a fool. "Now, David. If you want to live a life outside of prison, there are a few things that need to be taken care of for your new partners in crime. Haha!"

"What the hell do you want from me?"

"First of all, you'll suspend Agent Miles from the case, publicly. I want a special friend to know their mole was caught. After that, you will stop the raids against the Triads and focus your investigation once again on Kosher Nostra. Until the time is right, of course."

"What time?"

"The time we take down the Lombardi puttana."

"Why not take them down yourself and leave us to do our jobs?"

"David, you're clueless, aren't you?"

David stood there speechless, knowing he would end his career by doing this. He knew he must do whatever within his power to get to Jessica Lombardi before they do.

"Two hours, David. Press conference. Captain Rodgers will make sure Agent Miles is in attendance."

---

David was standing once again at the precinct's podium with the same crowd of fellow officers, law enforcement and media a few feet away from him. David called the local newspapers and told them he had a very important announcement to make at 3 PM. All other officers out on patrol were called into the precinct formally to support Special Agent Allen's press conference.

David stood at the edge of the platform looking like a complete mess; no tie and hair uncombed. He cleared his throat and the buzzing of the crowd stopped. "After a full night of probing and thorough surveillance…" David paused. His voice started to hoarse. He turned to the side, looking at Agent Miles for a moment who was standing next to Captain Rodgers. He had no idea what was going on. Not yet anyway.

"After nights of probing, the OC Task Force, in partnership with the 7th Police precinct of New York City, FBI and CIA have made an important step towards the unveiling the facts of our case against organized crime networks in New York City. Our results so far have been subpar to my standards, but this is not the fault of many of the exemplary officers who stand here in this room today. Those who come to work everyday risking their lives and families for keeping this city safe." David paused looking at Agent Miles who saw his eyes examining him. He sensed something wasn't right.

"However our shortcomings can be attributed to a single individual who unfortunately is here with us in this room today. The first day I came here I told you all that your precinct was corrupt, down to its core. I would never imagine that someone in my task force would be the same. But I'm not afraid to say this publicly, because I want truth and justice to prevail. Agent Tony Miles, come forward." The entire audience turned their eyes to him.

Miles stood there with his jaw dropped and his eyes widened. He didn't expect an outcome like this - a public shaming. "Agent Miles, now." David repeated and Miles slowly walked up like a zombie in a horror movie. "Until you are cleared, you will turn in your badge, gun, and passport, Agent Miles. You are under house arrest until further notice."

Miles handed in his gun and badge and took a long look at David. What he saw was sorrow in David's eyes. Miles then turned his back and started walking through the crowd with two officers. The officers present booed Miles, throwing papers and pens at him. It was a walk of shame. He knew half of those officers were dirty, but haven't gotten caught yet. The officers escorted Tony Miles out of the building where he was ambushed by a wave of reporters. *Who blackmailed you? How much were they paying you? Why did you do it? Will you testify?*

The questions were coming at him like bullets being fired from a machine gun. Miles pushed the reporters away as he was placed inside the unmarked police vehicle. Agent Miles knew his career in law enforcement was over.

"That is all." David said turning his back, ignoring the reporters. Meanwhile, the officers were shouting *"traitor"* repeatedly inside the lobby. David headed to his office with tears in his eyes. He betrayed the people he swore to serve and protect. The mob had broken him. He closed his eyes, falling asleep, hoping to never wake up again.

## LET'S MAKE A DEAL

Jessica walked through Chinatown around midday. The marketplace was crowded, with Chinese merchants and shoppers going from shop to shop. She was surrounded by four bodyguards clutching their Thompsons beneath their leather coats. The time for the mind games was a thing of the past. *Now, it was time for some real action.*

Three days passed since Agent Allen's press conference and the Triads became even fiercer. Jessica moved through the crowd which appeared to open for her to pass. She fixed her sunglasses, on her way to a small alleyway leading to Zhang's gambling house. She knocked on the door twice. Nobody answered and Jessica placed her ear on the door, hearing conversations between the Chinese arguing about a poker match. Jessica banged again but again no one answered.

"Open up. This is Jessica Lombardi, I'm here for Mr.

Zhang." she shouted and by luck, the door opened, revealing a dark room hidden behind it, brightened only by the flickering lights of candles and makeshift water fountains. Jessica nodded to her men to go in first. Their guns were out, but as soon as they were inside, the sounds of guns being loaded echoed the room.

Jessica followed them and saw they were surrounded by six Triads. Even some old men at the poker table pulled out their knives. "Stand down," a man at the door shouted in Chinese. He instructed Jessica and her men to follow him. "Wait here and don't fuck the bitches," Jessica said when they came to another area of poker tables and bikini-clad women looking seductive.

Leading the way, the man held the doors open for Jessica as they passed through hallways finally arriving at Mr. Zhang's office. The smell of Sweet Othmanus filled the air as she entered. Zhang was sitting behind his desk, taking a sip from a porcelain teacup. He gestured for Jessica to take a seat.

"Mr. Zhang, my name is-"

"I know who you are, Jessica Lombardi, daughter of the Don Michael. I was expecting you sooner."

Jessica glanced at a tea cup that Zhang had offered her.

"It's not poisoned, Jessica. I could have killed you downstairs."

Jessica grabbed the cup and took a sip, enjoying its richness.

"I'm here to make a deal with you, Mr. Zhang."

"I know why you are here. I know of your little police setup."

"So you do?"

"Unlike you, I wasn't born yesterday."

Jessica waved her hair, leaning closer to Zhang.

"Look, Zhang. In the last few months, I almost own over half of New York and…"

"Almost."

"And I won't stop now."

"So you want to go to war with me, Jessica?"

"I'm here to give you a chance. Alexander was smart enough to take it."

"Alexander had no other choice."

"Neither do you."

"My empire is a dynasty, Jessica. We have already taken over a big chunk of most of the petty gangs businesses and we are under the radar and protection of the NYPD."

"So you believe?"

"Jessica. This is the Triad life. We play the long game. That's why things are booming and can't be stopped. Hit us one time, it will do nothing. We're like a river, taking down with us those who destroyed the dam."

"I see. Accept my offer for protection and we can avoid a war, Mr. Zhang." Jessica felt trying to win an argument with Zhang was of no use.

"Look, Miss. Jessica. I have nothing against you. This is the game. I get it. And I respect you for your father's sake. But we are smarter, Jessica Lombardi. Never think I would hand over my empire to a woman with empty threats."

Jessica knew he was right and she was so close in taking over, she couldn't stop now. She felt disheartened but not crushed. *Leave this to your brother, Giovanni, my dear Jessica.* Her father's words were playing over and over in her head, like a broken record.

"Okay, Mr. Zhang. This will not be our last meeting. Mark my words." Jessica got up, storming out of the office.

"I hope not, Jessica. It was a very productive meeting." Zhang took another sip, watching Jessica's abrupt exit.

————

Jessica called for a meeting with all the family heads. It was time for the alliance to go on an all-out war against New York. They must show they run this city and no one else. Jessica lit up the last cigarette in the pack and balled-up the carton in anger.

The moment Jessica took her first drag, the door to her office opened and Sofia entered followed by the family heads. Sofia rushed taking a seat across Jessica. There was no time for greetings or celebrations. Everyone was silent, thinking about the pressing matter at hand.

In Jessica's mind existed one thing; war. There was nothing else to discuss.

"You might be aware by now that we have been put in a compromising position. Andrea, please brief us on what happened to Agent Miles?"

"The Feds found out the evidence we gave him was all bogus. He's on house arrest and now they are coming down harder on the streets."

"Damn! They will now focus on our gun and laundering operations," Sabina interrupted.

"Maybe. What about the Jews and Triads?" Jessica asked.

"Alexander seems to be safe but the Triads' money seem to have reached the hands of some officers on the force."

"Shit. If they get David Allen on their side, we're in a very tight spot," Julius mentioned.

Jessica continued, "By the way, I spoke with Zhang earlier. He's not willing to make a deal with us."

"Why would he be given a chance anyway? That makes us look weak, Jessica. It may have compromised us," Sabina argued.

"I know, Sabina. I was trying to avoid an all-out war. But it seems we have no other option."

"With all due respect, Donna Jessica, that was very foolish," Sabina continued.

"Then, we have to attack tonight. Zhang believes we are still negotiating. We will cripple his operations, the old-fashioned way before he finds out."

"I figured it would come to this, Signorina. That is why…" Julius opened his briefcase, taking out a file, sliding it towards her.

"What's this?"

"A train, Signorina. The Triads want access to our guns. They found an outside supplier and will bring in the first of shipments by train tonight."

"Sabina. Would you not like to take out our gun competitors for good?" Jessica asked hoping for her vote of confidence. It was the alliance's chance to show Zhang and other gangs they weren't messing around.

"I believe it is, Darling." Julius said handing the file to Sabina. "We're sitting on a deck of cards. One wrong card and we'll all be buried alive, Signorina."

"I agree. If we sit by and let them bring in these guns, we're doomed," Andrea exerted.

"Are we all in agreement?" Jessica asked.

Everyone nodded and Sabina grabbed the file, giving it a peek.

"Okay, I'm in," Sabina said. "But I want your help, Andrea. We could use some police maps." Sabina said passing the file to Andrea.

"Andrea, give Sabina what she needs. I want this matter with the Triads solved by midnight. Are we clear? Failure is not an option anymore."

Everyone at the table was on board. It was a risk fucking with the Triads but their trust in Jessica masked their insecurities.

"I know that the recent events have thrown us a little

behind schedule. I can reassure you all, if you believe in me and stand with me, there is nothing that can stand in our way. Thank you for giving me your pledges and commitment," Jessica said.

"That will be all. I'm expecting good news at midnight. You're dismissed."

Everyone left the room, talking to one other. Jessica didn't see Sofia anywhere until Sofia cleared her throat standing right behind her.

"Are you sure this will work, Jessica?"

"Why shouldn't it?"

"You must be smart now and angry later."

"I know Sofia, but some things require our immediate attention."

"Sometimes you must be like a slingshot, my Donna."

"What do you mean?"

"It means to fall back until the best moment to strike and then it will have a greater impact."

"I'm afraid that's not an option here."

"Why not? Because you are in a hurry for retaliation? When will this come to an end?"

"When I control everything, Sofia! Every single thing in this city."

Sofia stayed silent as Jessica was being blinded by her rage. Her ears were becoming deaf when taking the advice that the senior family heads were offering her. Jessica wanted an all-out war with the city; a war that Sofia knew they couldn't win.

Sofia got up and headed for the door. "Remember this, Donna Jessica. We all got here because of your intelligence."

## 26

## THE AMBUSH

The train station was clearing out. The last train had came and the passengers were exiting the station's platform. The sound of the train's engine echoed into the air as the conductor returned the train back to the yard for tomorrow.

Everyone had gone home, except for ten men, dressed in raincoats and ski masks. The men walked towards the platform, hiding their weapons inside their coats.

They stood at the platform like passengers for the next train coming. The lights at the train station's platform turned off signaling that the station was officially close down for the night. The men remained there, like ten dark silhouettes in the moonlight.

An half an hour went by and in the air, a train was heard approaching and in a matter of minutes, it docked on the platform waiting.

One of the men went around to the driver's door and tapped on the window. The driver, opened the door and the gunman entered pointing his Thompson at the driver. The internal door, connecting the control room with the A-class carriage opened and two Chinese men entered, pointing their guns. The man grabbed the driver and held his mouth shut as he tried to scream. His shrieks were constrained by the sounds of the men talking in Chinese. A few seconds later, the gunman was shot dead while the driver was also wounded. Upon hearing the gunshots, the group of men in ski masks ran up to the train, moved swiftly towards the wagons on the back of the train, opening the sliding doors, realizing that the hauls were empty.

Out of the dark, a dozen of Chinese men with Uzis appeared on the train platform, sneaking up behind the group of men wearing ski masks. A series of guns clicked and after a few moments, the station was barraged with bullet casings. Bodies of the men in masks were adding up. More Chinese appeared from inside the cargo wagon, shooting.

The ten men of Sabina had no chance. The intel from Julius mentioned there would only be the driver and maybe two Chinese guards onboard and a few crew workers waiting at the dock to unload the guns. Now, there were more than twenty on the scene while there appeared to be no shipment of guns -the perfect setup.

As Sabina's men got mowed down, everything went from gray to black. The station lit up flash after flash and a few minutes, the night's silence overtook the scene again.

## 27

## ILL FATE

Julius accompanied Jessica inside her office. Her hands were trembling like a person with Parkinson's. She struggled to light another cigarette while Julius stayed silent like a child inside the principal's office. He knew he was to blame for the failed operation.

"How could this go wrong?" Her words slivered out one at a time. Jessica was exhausted.

"We were given false information, Donna Jessica. Zhang's smarter than we thought."

"Zhang isn't smart. I was naïve, Julius."

"No my dear, Donna."

"Those fucking Triads disrespected us. Left our men bodies there with their dicks cut off. Now Sabina's morale is down."

"It seems that Zhang wanted to send us a message."

"Then we must send a message back."

"The Triads must have had some help on the inside."

"Who could have tipped them off?"

"I'm not sure if I can find out from our men on payroll in the precincts. Ever since, Agent Miles got singled out, everyone has been hushed."

"There's something else going on and it sounds like we have a bigger problem than the Triads."

"It looks like that might be the case, Donna Jessica."

"Knowing that *cazzo* Jacopo, I believe he is the one who might have help the Triads ambush our men."

"Since when does Italians go in bed with the Chinese?"

"Knowing Jacopo, he won't just stop there."

"What do we do about this?"

"Donna Jessica, you've brought us this far. Remember what I asked you the first time we spoke."

"If my head's in the game."

"Is it?"

"Yes and no."

"Please remain focused, Donna Jessica or these might be our last breaths."

Don Julius walked out of the room on his black shiny cane as Jessica sat in misery. A combination of the amount of cigarettes Jessica smoked that day, the ambush and now the possibly of Jacopo Saltinotti gaining power, she felt overwhelmed.

She wanted another drag from the cigarette but she put it out with disgust. Her lungs wanted to scream from being so close to the end and now everything was spiraling out of control like a rock falling from the top of a mountain.

A soft tap on the door brought her back to her senses. It was Alberto. "Jess, are you okay?" he said grabbing a chair and holding her hand.

"Yes, it's just…"

"Easy, my love." Alberto hugged her tightly pulling her closer. Jessica missed affection. She rested between his arms and cried.

"What's wrong, my love?"

"Everything."

"Can I help somehow?"

"If you can make the Triads disappear, that would be great."

"I wish I could. What's your plan?"

"I'm not sure I should be sharing any information outside of the alliance's circles, my love."

"You still don't trust your business with me, Jess? Hell, you trust me with your son," Alberto's said frustrated but his face look like a sad puppy.

"Stop doing that" Jessica smiled, kissing him. "My decision to attack the Triads at the train station went wrong last evening. All ten of our men died."

"You couldn't have known."

"Well, I could have been more wary."

"Well, now it's done. What will you do to fix it?"

"I will…" Jessica paused as her mind wandered. *Can I trust him even though he's my husband?*

"What are the Triads into?"

"Gambling, prostitution, sex toys, the whole nine."

"Haha, sex toys. So, let's say the Triads are making the most money in gambling, why not find a way to entice their big spenders to gamble with you?"

"That's smart, Alberto. For a man not in the business, you've pitched a good idea."

"It's just a thought."

"If I could get records on their high rollers, I could offer them higher payouts with some extras if they gamble with us. The Triads will have no choice but to bow down to us and Jacopo…."

"Jacopo Saltinotti?"

"Yeah, never mind. Forget I mentioned the stronzo's name."

"Well, okay."

"Tomorrow night, I'll organize a strike on every gambling spot the Triads have. We'll keep taking everything they have until Zhang is forced to give up."

"Thank you, Alberto. Give me a few minutes. I need to make a few calls."

"I'll be in the living room." Alberto closed the door behind him and Jessica called Julius back in to go over the logistics of each Triad gambling hideout. *There was no time to waste.* After dismissing Julius, Jessica tried going to the living room to see Alberto but felt weak.

Alberto spent the next thirty minutes alone in the living room. He heard Sofia washing the dishes after putting Luca to sleep. The sound of the cutlery and dishes soothed his mind. He waited and waited but

Jessica was still in her office. Alberto got up and went to the door. "Jess?" he whispered, but there was no answer. Alberto opened the door and saw Jessica lying face first on her desk. "Jess?" he whispered again.

Moving closer, he placed his hands on her shoulders. "You must be exhausted, Jess? Let me take you upstairs to bed?" he said chuckling, but Jessica still didn't respond. Her skin had turned pale and her breathing was slowing down. Alberto shook her, but Jessica didn't move. He checked her pulse, and it was faint. "Jess!" he screamed as he lifted her up.

Her eyes were rolled back, white as her skin. "For the love of Dio, Jess!" Alberto screamed trying to shake her awake. "Sofia! Call 911." Alberto shouted as Sofia's heavy footsteps approached the office.

"What's wrong Alb…" Sofia didn't complete her sentence dropping a glass of wine. "Oddio! What happened, Alberto?" Sofia shouted running towards the telephone. "She's barely breathing. I don't know!" Alberto shouted. He lifted Jessica carrying her to the living room sofa while Sofia dialed 911.

Alberto tried giving her CPR, but Jessica wasn't responsive although she was still alive. The sound of another set of footsteps were heard coming. "Is Mommy okay?" Luca asked standing at the top of the stairs, rubbing his eyes, awaken by the shouting.

"Yes, Luca. Mommy's just tired." Alberto tried comforting the kid. Luca came downstairs, rushing to his mother's side. "Why is so white?" Luca asked grabbing his mother's hand. "And cold."

"Mommy didn't eat her vegetables this morning," Alberto lied while listening to the desperation of Sofia's voice talking on the phone to the operator.

For the next ten minutes, Sofia tried helping Jessica while Alberto kept Luca busy. The young boy realized that something was wrong with his mother. The ambulance came and the medics took Jessica out on a stretcher, giving her oxygen. The ambulance drove as fast as it could through the dusk. "I'll get the car." Alberto said scared and pale as Jessica was.

"Go! But I'll drive." Sofia said taking Luca upstairs and getting him dressed. Sofia couldn't trust Alberto behind the wheel and felt it would be better for him to be in the back seat, calming down Luca. Alberto went to get the car and parked in front, honking the car's horn.

"Let's go." Sofia said to Luca carrying him outside. "Is Mommy going to be okay, Grandma?" Luca asked again. "Yes Luca. Mommy will be alright." Sofia strapped in the car seat. They drove off, almost catching up with the ambulance in route to the hospital.

Luca cried when he saw the ambulance's red lights realizing that something hurt his mommy. Alberto tried silencing him but to no avail. Sofia focused her attention on the road believing Jessica would be okay. *She must.* Jessica meant everything to the success of the Italians ruling New York.

Sofia and Luca were sitting in the hospital room with Jessica. The same hospital, Jessica wished she would never visit again. Luca had fallen asleep in Sofia's arms while her eyes were fixed on Jessica. Her mind blocked out the repetitive heart monitoring sound. She focused only on Jessica's breathing. The doctors placed a nasal cannula inside her nostrils, making her look gravely ill. Her skin was still pale but her heart rate had stabilized. Sofia felt better, taking a sip from the hot cocoa that Alberto had brought her.

It's been three hours since Jessica had been admitted. Sofia looked out the window, watching the dark empty street. No cars were passing by or people walking. "Hey, Sofia." Jessica moaned waking up. Sofia turned to her. Jessica's eyes were red, but she was alive. She rushed to her side and caressed her head.

"How are you feeling, Donna Jessica?"

"Like shit."

"You look like it." Sofia chuckled as Jessica returned a smile, sheltering her pain.

"What happened to me?"

"You passed out."

"When?"

"Alberto found you. You were lying on your desk. You scared us to death."

"Where's Alberto? He went home to check on things. I'll call him now you are awake."

"What did the doctors say?"

"They took a blood sample and had done a few more tests. We're waiting for the results to come back."

Jessica smiled closing her eyes, struggling to ignore the pain in her chest. Sofia walked back to her seat, allowing Jessica to get more rest. After thirty minutes, a doctor entered. "Miss. Jessica Lombardi?" He asked.

"That's me," said Jessica slowly opening her eyes. The doctor looked around the room and nodded to Sofia. "Take the child outside for a little while, Ma'am. Thank you. I will need to speak to Miss. Lombardi alone." Sofia nodded holding Luca who was still asleep and carrying him outside. Then the door shut while the doctor turned to Jessica with sorrow in his eyes.

"Miss. Lombardi."

"Give me the bad news first, Doctor."

"I'm not sure how to put this."

"In plain English." Jessica mocked, trying to keep a cold-hearted boss appearance.

"I'm afraid you to tell you but you have lung cancer and it's in the advanced stages."

Jessica smiled as if she didn't have a worry in the world.

"Okay, tell me the bad news, Doctor."

"I'm afraid that this is the bad news. Your smoking habit is perhaps the cause, but we can't tell for sure..." the doctor kept explaining. A soft buzz met her ears and her head started spinning. Each word that came out of the doctor's mouth was sinking her deeper in a slumber.

Everything was becoming dark around her. She heard the doctor's words which sounded like whispers, but she couldn't turn it off and fell back asleep.

An hour later, Jessica opened her eyes again and saw Sofia and Luca standing next to her. The doctor was not in the room.

"Sofia? What happened?"

"You passed out again."

"The doctor…said in a few months, I'll be….," slurred Jessica.

Sofia's eyes flooded with tears. Luca didn't know what she was talking about. "Are you going to be okay, Mommy?" He asked grabbing her hand. Jessica held back her tears, grabbing his. "Yes, sweetheart. I just forgot to eat my vegetables. That's all." Jessica coincidentally lied like Alberto and it felt bad.

"Are you sure, Mommy?"

"Yes, baby.. That's what the doctor told me before. To eat my vegetables every day." Jessica smiled as tears ran down her face.

"Why are you crying then?" Luca quizzed squeezing her hand tighter.

"I just woke up from a nightmare I had, Baby and I'm glad you are here to save me," said Jessica hugging him. Sofia and Jessica exchanged a long look. They knew they had to stay strong for each other for Luca's sake.

Sofia approached and joined in the hug with Jessica. The women didn't speak on the matter further and Sofia felt devastated for Jessica.

"Luca, sweetheart. Show Mommy what you found in Alberto's car."

Luca nodded and skipped towards the chairs, returning with a big old photo album.

"Come here and sit down," said Jessica tapping on a spot next to her on the bed. Sofia helped little Luca up. Luca opened the album on his lap almost as big as him. "Look Mommy, that's me when I was little," said Luca pointing at a a photo from his first nursery.

"Yes, honey. That was back in Italy," said Jessica as they flipped through the pages.

"Is Italy far from here?"

"Yes, honey. Very. But we will visit there soon. It's very beautiful and it's our home."

They kept going through the photo album, looking at all the pictures from the day; Luca walked for the first time, Jessica's and Alberto's wedding, and while they were vacationing in Milan.

"Look Mom, that's my school." Luca said. "I will go back to school right?" he asked worried. "You will, Baby. No matter what, you must not skip a day of school unless you are sick like Mommy, alright?"

"Yes, Mom."

They kept browsing until Jessica noticed something weird about the photos. "Luca, Mommy needs you to the bathroom and see if there are any paper towels." Jessica looked at Sofia.

"Yes, Mommy." Luca jumped off the bed.

"What is it, Jessica?"

"Sofia. Look." Jessica turned the album towards her, pointing at photos of Luca.

"He is gorgeous, isn't he?"

"You're missing something. Oddio! that bastard. Where is he?"

"Who?"

"Alberto!"

"Home. Why?"

"Look at this, Sofia."

Sofia looked at the pictures, one by one.

"O dio mio!"

Jessica grabbed the photos out of the book that didn't belong. Someone was taking pictures of Jessica and Luca and it wasn't Alberto.

"That's me and Julius. And me with Alexander Lavie. And me, in Kynami's office. Look at you with Andrea outside the school. That's the family heads entering our home for a meeting."

"*Brutto figlio di puttana!*"

"That *bastardo* Alberto is working for Jacopo or the police."

"This is crazy, Jessica."

"If these photos have ended up in NYPD's hands, we'll be in dead or in prison for life."

"How could this be?"

"Alberto has these photos for a reason. I can only imagine what else he has on me."

"He won't be able to lie once he comes back from home."

"He's not coming back. Call our men to get ready." Jessica said getting out of bed.

"Are you sure… your health?"

"Oh, I'm fine now. Alberto's fucking dead!" Jessica stormed to the phone outside the door and dialed her house number. She was tapping her leg when Luca came out with the paper towels.

"Here, Mommy. I brought you plenty."

"Thank you, sweetheart," said Jessica pretending everything was alright.

"Why are you standing up?"

"I'm just calling Alberto. Mommy needs something from home."

Sofia took out pieces of paper and crayons from her bag, handing them to Luca. "Here Luca, why don't you make Mommy a nice picture?"

"Okay, Grandma." Luca said sitting on the marble floor, drawing with his crayons.

Jessica looked at Sofia with a menacing stare. "He is not fucking picking up."

She kept dialing and still there was no answer.

"Call the family and our men," whispered Jessica.

"Surely, Donna Jessica. Right away," Sofia whispered back.

"Fuck!" Jessica was disgusted.

"What is it? Are you in pain?"

"No, I remembered something else."

"What?"

"Before I passed out, I was in the office going over

some details about going after the Triads' gambling rings with Alberto."

"What?"

"Alberto knows all about it and when."

"Oh shit! Donna Jessica."

Jessica flopped on the bed, exhausted. Just like that she got outsmarted by the Triads and the Saltinottis. With Alberto working against her and her ordeal with advanced stage cancer, Jessica craved for a cigarette knowing it would only kill her off faster. For now, she had to respond quickly or else, the empire would crumble to pieces.

## 28

## THE TRAITOR

Alberto was walking down a dark street and it was too late for anyone to be outside. Walking alone and lost in thoughts, he was holding what resembled a large book in his hands. The moonlight seemed to follow Alberto's footsteps and a dog's barking in the distance disturbed the normal neighborhood's silence. As Alberto walked by, the more barks could be heard.

He looked around at the matching houses seeing beautiful yards, white fences, and children's' toys left outside in the front yards. This was his ultimate dream; to have a modern home, beautiful wife and one healthy son. Alberto didn't sense living in the life of organized crime, nor its grime. Somehow, he got caught up with someone who was the main archenemy of the New York's Lombardi family.

At the end of the street, a mansion with a porch light

shined. It reminded him of a lighthouse at the end of an ocean's coastline. Alberto walked faster. The yard of that mansion was behind a metal fence and two guards stood outside, concealing their guns. Alberto saw three spotlights turning in sync, scanning the yard. The place resembled a king's fortress.

The guards stopped him raising their arms. "Arresto." a man on the right said. "Chi sei? Cosa fai qui?" the man yelled at Alberto.

"I'm Alberto Saltinotti. I'm family and here to see my cugino, Jacopo."

The guards lowered their guns recognizing Alberto. "Mi dispiace. Filleto, Signore Alberto," said one of the guards pressing a button on the side of the gate.

A repetitive buzz echoed, followed by the two iron doors opening like the gate of a castle. Alberto walked between the guards without saying a single word up to the porch and opened the front door. Alberto's guilt kicked in feeling bad that he didn't stay at the hospital with Jess. Once he realized his mistake of Luca taking the photo album from his car, he knew he couldn't turn back.

Alberto entered the living room where Jacopo was sitting in front of a fireplace, drinking a glass of Barbera. Beside him were David Allen of the OC Task Force and Mr. Zhang, the leader of the Triads. Jacopo's eyes widened when he saw Alberto enter the living room.

"Cugino!" Jacopo called out, kissing Alberto with respect on the cheeks.

"Jacopo…"

"Why the sad face, cugino?"

"Jessica's in hospital."

"Still worrying about that puttana?"

"Hey. Watch it cugino, that's my wife."

"She's in the past, Alberto. Did you bring me what I asked for?"

"Here it is. "Alberto handed him the large book.

"Excellent. Agent Allen, look at this and tell me if it's enough for a warrant."

"Jacopo. You promised me. No killing."

"Okay, okay. She'll end up in jail for life. Will that make you feel better, Alberto?"

"Yes, it would."

"I still can't understand how you fell for her."

"I spent the last four years with her, Jacopo."

"You were there to spy on her, not to fall in love."

"That wasn't my fault, but…."

"Weak men."

"Don't fucking touch her, cugino. Make sure she goes to prison. New York is already yours."

"Watch your mouth, Alberto."

"Are you going to kill me, cugino? We're famiglia, remember. Haven't you killed enough people?"

"Cugino!" Jacopo smiled, trying to hide his temper. "I get it. You're angry. Betraying your wife, that is bad. It was the plan all along. That's why I got you the documents for your green card and that's why I sent you to

Italy. You were my insurance plan, in case, the Lombardi *puttana* came back."

"Sorry to interrupt, gentlemen. Just a little family dispute," continued Jacopo.

"I see," laughed Zhang while David stayed silent.

"Give me a fucking drink," Alberto yelled. One of Jacopo's men came forward to pour him a glass of Barbera.

*Would it be easy to leave the woman of his life for the past four years? A life that was built upon a lie? Alberto Caruso was destined to be the country's leading civil engineer but no longer.*

Zhang enjoying his wine while Agent Allen stared over the photos that were inside the large book. "It's more than enough to put her away forever," claimed Agent Allen.

"*Perfetto!*" Jacopo smiled taking a long sip.

"Did you remove your things, Alberto?"

"I took everything including my underwear."

The men laughed including David Allen who did so under duress.

"*Ottimo lavoro!* Any more information about Jessica and her family bandits?"

"She thinks you are in bed with Triads and will order a strike later this evening on every gambling site of Mr. Zhang's."

"I didn't expect that. It would be smart but we are smarter than her, of course."

The men laughed again with the exception of David.

"Agent Allen. Handle this my friend. I want every

officer on your force to arrest anyone near Mr. Zhang's gambling businesses. Mr. Zhang, as promised, your gambling sites are safe with me."

"You have finally delivered your promise, Jacopo."

"Jacopo—excuse me. I will get going," said David getting up and leaving while Jacopo was boasting about his progress so far.

As the night when on, Alberto's mind was solely on Jessica. Internally, he tried justifying his betrayal but couldn't find any excuse. Alberto loved her but not enough.

## 29

# THE CHINATOWN MASSACRE

The streets of Chinatown were as busy as ever with the incomprehensible talking of its residents. No one understood what was going on except those who lived there. The shouting between the merchants and customers sounded like arguments between siblings. The streets' clubs and bars were overcrowded and the restaurants were full. Well-dressed businessmen combed the area but most were not there for the ordinary shopping reasons. They were there for the illegal casinos located in the backs of department stores. The big spenders, loan sharks and prostitutes all were looking to make a fortune.

The overcrowded market was then rattled by black Cadillacs coming through the crowd like a ships cruising in the deep seas. Over twenty Cadillacs, along with ten black vans with black-tinted windows and no license plates swarmed the area. Over seventy men dressed in black raincoats, with their faces covered got out of the vehicles, loading their shotguns.

Chaos quickly spread through Chinatown as more and more men appeared going from one shop to another. They were prepared to invade. Sabina Baldinotti was standing among them, screaming orders at the top of her young lungs in Italian. Just like that, the entire marketplace was empty, like an old deserted town. Only the Italians were there, ready to take over Triad territory.

Andrea made sure to bribe the police officers beforehand, assuring that the hit wouldn't be interrupted. The legions of men began breaching the shops, at once, shooting the ceilings as the men and women inside, crouched under tables.

The sounds of screaming overtook the scene as Sabina's men threatened the shop owners, forcing entry to the casinos in the back. Every shop was sabotaged and in a matter of minutes without bloodshed, Sabina was in charge of Zhang's territory.

With only the main office of Zhang left to be breached, Sabina dashed up an dark alleyway in the back of the largest store with a few of her men. To her surprise, the office door was left open. With a single signal of her hand, two of her men including Carl loaded their guns and broke down the door to Zhang's office. The place was empty. The men shrugged and kept moving. Sabina with two others followed the first group cautiously, taking slow steps.

"Where's everyone?" Sabina complained. "Search

everything." she yelled and everyone spread out, flipping tables, searching for Zhang's stashes.

Sabina spotted another staircase on a second level and proceeded to it with Carl and another. The door was left open as well. She pushed the handle, holding her shotgun upwards, close to her lips. The office was left empty. No furniture, no decorations, nothing. The building appeared to be abandoned. Sabina sensed something was wrong. She turned around and before she took three steps backwards, a gunshots echoed the building. Sabina and her men took cover.

A barrage of gunshots rang, making the area shake. Sabina remained down as the sound of everything being torn to pieces and her men getting hit terrified her. She peeked outside the window and saw blue and red lights flashing down the dark alleyway. Sabina was holed up and heard heavy footsteps approaching her.

She made the sign of the cross on her chest and when the footsteps were only but a few feet away, she aimed to shoot. "No!" One of the huge bodyguards yelled. "Donna Sabina, we've been setup. The place is empty and the police…." the man panted.

*"Sabina Baldinotti. Surrender now and no one has to die,"* a voice shouted on a loud speaker.

"What the hell is going on down there?" Sabina asked terrified.

"The fucking pigs killed most of our men."

"Fuck."

To the sound of the man's words, Sabina felt as if

everything around her was spinning, like a carousel going faster and faster. She grabbed the Carl's shoulder regaining her balance.

"Donna Sabina, let's go!" Carl said with confidence loading his gun. Sabina opened her mouth but a dozen heavy footsteps coming up the stairs interrupted her. "I guess it's too late," said Sabina loading her weapon to make one last stand.

"It was a pleasure," said Carl ready to shoot. Before his hand could touch the trigger, repetitive flashes lit up the room. Dozens of bullets struck Carl's big body. More holes than Sabina had ever seen in her life.

FBI agents swarmed the area. "Sabina Baldinotti, drop it!" shouted the agent in charge, pointing his semi-automatic towards her. "I'm sorry, Father," she said raising her gun. Before she could fire, a series of bullets struck her in the head. In a single moment, she was dead.

———

The FBI were disguised as Saltinotti men eliminated Sabina and her men. The setup was to draw Sabina and her men inside to trap them where they would have no chance of escape. Jessica's plan again had failed. Jacopo had the inside-track on how to make her plan crumble like a huge pile of ash.

After the melee, the FBI agents and OC Task Force, under the orders of Special Agent Allen, dragged the bodies to the middle of Chinatown, where a large pile was formed from the dozens of bodies including Sabina. David stood in front of his OC agents and the Saltinotti men disguised as FBI agents, with sadness in his eyes. He had just committed the most atrocious act in his life. This would follow him for the rest of his career in law enforcement and destroy him. It was his *Bloodshed*.

"Good job, men. Tonight, we made a big leap towards restoring order in the city of New York. Bringing back law and order from these criminals like you see laying dead in these piles," shouted David and everyone clapped. The men sought morale from his words. Jacopo's men were armed and ready to kill again. His agents believed they were doing the right thing, but David knew the truth.

David then walked off heading to an empty area and dialed Jacopo's number. As the phone rang, he attempted to hold in his frustration.

"Si?" Jacopo answered. "It's fucking done." David said with tears running down his face. He was more guilty than those who were killed.

"*Ben fatto!* Send your agents home, but I want you to stay there and wait for my orders." Jacopo then hung up.

David turned around and shouted to his men. "Time to clear out. The FBI is taking over the operation from this point forward." His men congratulated him, leaving while the Salnottis stayed behind with David.

## 30

## NO MORE SOLDATO

J acopo hang up the phone and turned around smiling at Zhang who was sitting at the edge of his seat waiting to hear the some good news.

"So?"

"It is done. The Baldinottis are history." Jacopo shook Zhang's hand.

"This calls for a celebration."

Jacopo headed to the shelve pulling off a bottle of 'Belle époque 61'. "I saved this for a special occasion like this." The Don opened the wine with respect, bearing something sacred.

He filled three glasses and offered one to Alberto who was sitting away from the men appearing sadden by the news. "Cheer up, Alberto. Your wife wasn't there." Jacopo said pouring another glass for Zhang. Zhang looked up at Jacopo like a fan in front of a famous rock star. "To many more victories." Jacopo raised his glass and Zhang followed.

Alberto didn't touch his glass. He kept sitting silently, sick to death of his cugino, Jacopo. So much bloodshed and Alberto was the traitor behind all of it.

"To you!" Zhang said happily.

"I have to admit, Jacopo, I didn't believe you could pull this off." Zhang said dancing in his seat. "So what's next?"

"Send your men back in. They can resume normal operations and tomorrow, we will continue forward. We don't want to lose any money, do we?"

Zhang stood up and dialing a number on his phone. He waited a few seconds and when someone answered, Zhang instructed, "Send everyone back in. It's over. God Bless, Jacopo."

"I am the Godfather of New York and there is nothing that can stand in my way," boasted Jacopo.

"Don't get full of yourself, Jacopo. I am still in control of the gambling rings."

"I know and that's why…"Jacopo pulled out his gun swiftly and shot Zhang three times. Zhang's eyes widened as he fell back on the sofa. His glass dropped on the floor, spilling wine everywhere and his mouth was coughing up blood.

"Why?" Zhang sputtered.

"Don't tell me you really believed I would get in bed with the Triads, Mr. Zhang!" Jacopo laughed. Alberto stood up in shock as his jaw dropped seeing Zhang's blood mix with the wine on the floor. "Jacopo? What the fuck?" shouted Alberto.

"Don't be a puttana, Alberto. He had it coming."

"Why kill him if he did what you asked?"

"The Italians only do business with their own and never do they trust petty crooks like Zhang."

Alberto stood still and couldn't believe what had just happened. He couldn't believe he was working for a man that got him to betray his own wife.

"Clean this up!" Jacopo said resting back in his arm chair, hitting the 'on' button on the radio - Beethoven Sonata No.1. Jacopo smiled as the sweet sound of the piano filled the room. Two men came forward to wrap the body in a sheet as Alberto reluctantly looked on.

Jacopo picked up the phone and called David Allen. Within seconds, David answered "Yes?"

"The Triads are coming to take back their casinos. Kill them all. And those who don't die, tell them they will be working for me now on. Oh, yeah and make sure you arrest a few if you can," Jacopo laughed.

"You can't be fucking serious."

"Do I sound like I'm in a mood for jokes, David? How would you feel if I share your dirt with the FBI?"

"It's not my dirt."

"Oh, it will be. Let me know how it goes."

David hanged up the phone and went to the Saltinottis in FBI uniforms waiting for his instructions. "Okay. Jacopo wants you to take out the Triads the moment they come back?" shouted David. The

Saltinottis were briefed on where to take positions. Jacopo already had this planned. *"Why does he need me?"* David mumbled taking position in a dark alleyway nearby.

———

Chinatown was painted red, with small rivers of blood flowing at every direction from the big pile of bodies in its middle. After a few minutes, Triad members showed up, heading to center to inspect the pile. They wanted to piss on the bodies and mock the dead Italians. That was their biggest mistake. As more and more turned up, the Saltinottis stood by in the dark alleys surrounding the scene, waiting David Allen's orders to attack.

David looked at the moon and pondered on why he was going against his oath for the system he swore to protect and serve all these years. He felt like a piece of trash as he peaked down the street with his binoculars and saw more Triads gathering around. He loaded his gun and began walking signaling to his men to get ready.

With each step, his boots plunged deeper into the blood that was left behind when the bodies were dragged. His tactical armor was already covered in blood. When he turned the corner, a voice of a Triad echoed. "Grenade!" A moment later, his voice got muffled by the explosion. The Saltinottis had already started attacking.

Gasoline was poured in a circle around the bodies before the Triads arrived. The explosion was followed by gunshots from different directions and blasts rocked the center of Chinatown. The scene resembled a concerto of fireworks.

David stood still with his gun in his hands, unable to shoot. He wasn't willing to take part in this and watched the Triads get slaughtered in front of his eyes. There wasn't anything he do to stop the massacre.

The gunfight lasted less than three minutes and most of the Triads were dead close to pile of Baldinottis. Those who weren't, kneeled on the ground and begged for their lives in Chinese. The guns of the Saltinottis were pointed at their heads.

David walked up to the scene and said, "Listen up" like a colonel shouting at his men in the army, crossing his hands behind his back. "This work is for Jacopo Saltinotti," David shouted and a soft roar followed. "Now, clean up the scene," said David obviously tired of the bullshit. He walked away from the madness. As long as it wasn't the police, he didn't feel much remorse.

The Saltinottis in FBI uniforms removed the piles of the Triads and the Italians in separate bulldozers. The remaining Triads were executed as Jacopo told his men to leave no witnesses behind.

## 31

## A STAUNCH WARNING

Jessica was sitting once again behind her desk, lost in her thoughts. The burning inside her chest had subsided but she knew what was behind the pain; the cancer. She didn't take her health into consideration when running things and did what she could to try to outsmart her rival, Jacopo.

When Michael was alive, Jessica did her best to try to prove her worth, running errands for father unlike her brother, Giovanni who was her father's muscle. Whatever Michael needed taken care of, Giovanni had a hand in on it. Similar to her late husband, Francesco who was the eldest male of the Guilani household. Jessica possessed a combination of all three men and many praised her for her bravery in making difficult decisions. But now, she started to believe people were praising her because no one was ready to step up, believing that they couldn't succeed.

Defeated as she was, the rage inside her was now slipping out. Jessica was trying to restore order at a time which was most crucial.

The phone rung, pulling her out of her endless daydreams. "Yes?" Jessica picked up the phone.

"I advise you, Signorina to turn on the news," the voice of Julius sounded with pity.

"Why?"

"What's going on can't be described with words, Donna Jessica." Jessica could feel something was deeply wrong.

"Is it that bad?"

"Worse, I'm afraid." A silence that lasted close to a minute as Jessica searched for the TV remote and finally finding it.

"Which channel?"

"Every," replied Julius.

The moment the news station came on, the receiver from Jessica's hand dropped.

"Jessica?" Julius' voice sounded like a man who had fallen into a well.

Jessica was in a state of shock as she looked at the aerial shots from news station's helicopter report from Chinatown. *The Bloodshed Part 2* was the headline of every news channel.

Jessica, without even taking her eyes from the screen, put a cigarette in her mouth and lit it up. Sitting frantically, she couldn't fathom the images displayed on the television. *Graphic content, please take your minors under the age of 13 away from the television.* Warnings appeared as the station's helicopter zoomed in on the pile of corpses.

Every public service department in New York City were called to respond at the Chinatown incident. Firemen were putting out fires while police were trying to keep everyone back from contaminating the crime scene. The city's morgue workers were tasked with picking up the dozens of bodies laying around. The scenes resembled a scene from World War II. Jessica slowly put the phone receiver back to her ear.

"Julius. I've failed you, all."

"It is not your fault, Signorina. We got outsmarted."

"No, it's my responsibility to lead us to victory."

"You couldn't foresee this, Signorina Jessica."

"I know what the reason for my failures. It has to do with my husband Alberto. He's working for Jacopo."

A pause followed as Julius tried taking in Jessica's words. "Are you sure?"

"Yes. I discussed with him some details in regards to our plan to invade the Triad hideout yesterday."

"I don't…"

"It's only a minor setback. We may have lost the battle but not the war," said Jessica taking a long drag of her cigarette. "I feel sorry for Sabina. Oh Dio"

"Julius?!" Jessica shouted. "Where's Sabina?"

"I'm afraid she didn't make it."

"Oh, no!" Jessica kept repeating. "I've failed her."

"It's not your fa-" Julius sentence was interrupted as Jessica abruptly hung up the phone.

*"One of the most gruesome incidents, New York City has ever faced. The OC Task Force are not able to give a statement at this time and it seems that no one is willing to talk—"* the young reporter said on the television. Jessica muted the TV, knowing who was behind all this.

———

Jessica's now under pressure to deal with the treachery of her husband Alberto, her health and an empire which appears to be crumbling. *What else could go wrong?*

Before finishing her cigarette, there seemed to be commotion at the front door. A moment of silence and Sofia's screaming made Jessica alarmed. She opened the top drawer and grabbed her Smith and Wesson. Staring ahead, she aimed, determined to strike anyone who would enter through that door. *Behold, it was Jacopo, the new godfather of New York.*

"Buonasera, Signorina." Jacopo bowed.

"Jessica, I'm sorry. I tried to stop him." Sofia yelled.

"It's okay, Sofia. Go check on Luca, please." Jessica hissed staring deeply into Jacopo's eyes, clutching her gun with her finger itching above the trigger.

Jacopo smiled as he walked in slowly inspecting every little detail inside. "I always wondered how Michael's office looked," Jacopo said mockingly.

"It's my office now."

"Oh it is but for how long?"

"Until I wipe your little ass off the face of the Earth."

"Do you have enough time?" Jacopo asked with his back turned to Jessica, inspecting an old vase on the bookcase.

"What are you implying, Jacopo?"

"Cancer is a nasty disease, isn't it?"

"What do you know about that?"

"So I hear. I don't know." Jacopo took the vase, inspecting it closely like a collector.

"Put that down."

"Finely crafted. Florence, I see?"

"Put it down now, Jacopo."

"16th century, I assume." Jacopo chuckled placing the vase back. "Don't worry. Alberto doesn't know about your health issues, but I know. I own this city; the hospitals, the police, everything."

"Since when?"

"Since the day Alberto started working for me?"

"What?"

"That was the day you first met in mother Italy."

"You're a lying bastardo!"

"Sounds weird, right?"

"How come?"

"I figured that Michael's bambina would return to New York one of these days. I needed someone to keep tabs on my dear lady. You are proving tougher than I expected. I probably should have killed my cugino,

Alberto by now and let him rot in a dumpster. But he's famiglia."

"What if your plan for us to fall in love didn't work?"

"Oh, that wasn't my first option. I knew you would need someone to comfort you after the death of Francesco. It's hard for a widow with a child to live the rest of her remaining days on Earth alone. Actually, Alberto was my third choice."

"The third?"

"Yes, you see. There were a few men who entertained the prospect of meeting you but the first two I found out I couldn't trust. They were too handsome and loved women too much. Therefore, I decided my cugino, Mr. Caruso was the best man for you."

In a single day, Jessica's world had fallen apart. Her marriage was fake, Sabina's dead and Jacopo invaded her privacy. Jessica stared at Jacopo who grabbed the best chair in the room and sat down.

"How dare you come inside my home?"

"I didn't come here for idle talk but I'm here to warn you. Some call me a psychopath, but I have honor as you see. At least for us, Italians."

"What does that mean?"

"Zhang's dead. Alexander would follow him soon when I find that slippery bastard. And Sabina unfortunately got caught in the wrong place at the wrong time."

"So you work for the Triads, now?"

"The Italians only work with their own, Miss.

Lombardi. Unless they're weak, they'll go make a shitty deal with Kosher Nostra or the fucking Triads."

Jessica tried maintaining her composure.

"This is where you almost wrecked my plan, Jessica. Congratulazioni." Jacopo chuckled picking up an old pen lying at the far right end of the table.

"We're not finished, Jacopo."

"Oh, yes we are. You see, I'm here to give you one chance and one chance only. Leave now and you can live the rest of your life in peace. You can take a few chemo-therapy sessions or whatever. Maybe you can outlive all of us."

"Or?"

"Or I'll speed things up and kill you off before your cancer does."

Jessica loaded her gun and placed it on top of her desk. "What stops me from killing you right now?"

"Aren't you madre of the year? Don't you care about little Luca?"

"Don't you ever say his name again."

"Or what?"

"I'll fucking kill you."

"Go ahead. My men will burn this house down with you and everyone inside." Jacopo put the pen down. His eyes were red as fire.

"Another word and I swear to God, I'll put a bullet between your eyes." Jessica stood up, pointing the gun at the Jacopo's head. Jacopo stood up opening his arms, inviting her.

"Come on." Jacopo said leaning closer. "Are you afraid to be me?" said Jacopo taunting her. "Or are you scared for Luca and Giovanni? I am so comfortable with the thought of death. Something you will never have. I have accomplished what you wished to, Jessica Lombardi?" As Jacopo kept pushing her, Jessica's hand kept shaking. The man had a talkative way of getting to his enemies, knowing when to push the right buttons at the right time.

Jacopo leaned closer and grabbed Jessica's gun, placing it on his forehead. "One pull of this trigger and everything you have will turn to dust. Think about it." Jacopo smiled. Jessica wanted Jacopo dead, but he was right. While she had the chance to end it all, Jessica wasn't ready to destroy her empire, family and dreams at once.

Jacopo lowered the gun, placing it back on Jessica's desk.

"That's what I thought. You have 24 hours to leave New York," said Jacopo leaving the office.

Jessica cried, unable to contain her tears. Jacopo didn't even flinch at the sight of death and that terrified her. He proved she was weak. With a single conversation, her entire plan was thrown in the trash. Jessica put her weapon back in the drawer.

Sofia stood by the doorstep, watching Jessica cry like the day she cried when she lost Francesco. Sofia didn't hear a word that Jacopo said, but she knew for sure he sure broke her.

## 32

## THE RAID

A day had passed and Jessica had disregarded Jacopo's notice. She spent her day with Luca, inside the house, drawing and playing board games. Jessica was compelled to spend as much time with as possible. The other family heads tried reached her many times, but she ignored everyone's calls. Sofia was sitting at the telephone, lying to everyone who called.

Jessica kept staring at Luca, with her eyes kept watering every time he laughed and smiled. He didn't go to school that day. Jessica felt it would safer for him to stay at home, away from danger.

After an hour of playing games and having fun, Luca was sound asleep lying on the couch while Jessica combed his hair. Sofia kept looking at them, thinking of a picture that reminded her of her two sons.

The atmosphere was heavy inside the Lombardi mansion. Sofia stayed silent and Jessica tried to avoiding eye contact with her. They knew if they talked to each another, a stream of bad news would drown them like a waterfall. Sofia ordered guards stay posted outside the mansion, in case Jacopo made due on his promise. The time went graciously into the evening without a sign of trouble.

———

It was a few minutes past midnight and Jessica carried Luca to his room, covering him in his favorite red blanket, the one they bought right before leaving Italy.

Jessica walked back downstairs coming to the living room where Sofia was having a glass of wine and smoking a cigarette. "Since when did you start smoking?" Jessica chuckled sitting next to Sofia, forgetting her misery for the moment.

"How much harm can one cigarette do?" Sofia coughed as the smoke crept down her throat.

"Jessica, are you nervous?"

"I am." Jessica said taking a sip of wine. Her hands were cold and shaking but she couldn't do anything about it.

"What are you afraid of?" asked Sofia. These weren't random questions that someone would ask.

"Losing you. Losing Luca."

"I think you're afraid to go down." Sofia answered. Jessica noticed that Sofia had a little too much to drink. It was the first time she saw Sofia drunken.

"I might be. Why's that wrong?"

"Don't you think it's time to give up and let…?"Sofia said before being interrupted.

"We came back for a reason, remember?"

"I remember Jessica but-"

"Remember the reason why we escaped to Italy?"

"I do and will do anything to avenge for my son and husband's death."

"That is why I'm here, Sofia."

"That was before. We tried taking New York and it's just a matter of time before Jacopo becomes boss. Why don't we just leave?"

"And let Jacopo ruin our names forever?"

"Our names will alway be cemented in New York's legacy."

Jessica remained silent. Sofia was right. Deep down inside, she realized they must leave but her pride was preventing her from seeing the truth.

"Why are you suddenly against me?"

"I'm not but I'm afraid, Jessica. Not for me and not for you. But for our little boy, Luca upstairs. I don't want him to end like our men."

Jessica stayed speechless. The strong woman, Sofia, that always supported her for the past five years sounded as if she was throwing in the towel. Jessica finished her drink and wasn't ready to give up. Not yet. Jessica opened her mouth to speak, but only a gasp slipped out of her mouth. "Sofia, slowly turn off the lights!"whispered Jessica.

Four green rays were moving in patterns outside the room's window.

"Dio Santo!" whispered Sofia.

Jessica pointed to Sofia to go upstairs and get Luca. She then crawled on the floor to get back to her office. Her gun was still sitting on the desk and she reached for it, not making a sound. By then, Sofia was by the steps ready to creep up the stairs.

Three sparks lit up from outside the window followed by three short yells. Their men appeared to be struck by silencers. Sofia gasped covering her mouth when they heard the thumps. Her gun was in her purse upstairs. The shadows of four of Jacopi's men walking up to the house suddenly appeared. Their footsteps on the gravel were loud enough to be heard.

Jessica saw a man in front of the window, looking inside. Without thinking, she pulled the trigger and the bullet hit the man's chest. Sofia ran upstairs, heading for Luca's room, while Jessica took cover behind the door. *"Man down!"* a man yelled. Seconds later, a battering ram hit the door with tremendous force but it wouldn't open.

"Cover me." the wounded man shouted and a can was thrown at the window, breaking it. A white smoke rapidly spread throughout the first floor. Jessica's eyes began turning red and her breathing got heavier. Another hit of the battering ram and the door broke down, followed by the sound of three sets of heavy footsteps marching inside.

The green rays pierced the white fog, scanning for

their target. Jessica crept towards the staircase, pointing her gun at the bottom of the stairs. "Clear," shouted one man. Jessica made it to Luca's room with Sofia and shut the door behind her. Luca was wide awake and ready to cry. Sofia held him tightly in her arms, covering his mouth.

Jessica placed her ear on the door, listening to men talking. "Clear," another shouted. "This is one's clear, sir," the voice of another could be heard. Jessica counted the rooms they had breached, keeping her ear tighter against the door. Then she heard another set of footsteps coming up the staircase.

She was running out of time. Jessica turned around and went towards Luca's window, pushing it open. "Let's go. I'll try to buy us some time," she whispered to Sofia.

"I'm not leaving you here, Jessica to be slaughtered by these Saltinotti pigs," argued Sofia as she held Luca.

"Sofia! Go now!" whispered Jessica as she pointed her gun towards the door.

Sofia knew that every second mattered and Jessica wouldn't change up her mind. They climbed out of the window, walking on the side of the house. Little Luca was stepping with his bare feet on the cold wet roof. "Just make it out alive. I'll be waiting for you in the garage," said Sofia.

Jessica kept staring at the door pushing the dressers and what she could find in front of the door. She heard the next room's door breached and the men were about to go to the room where Jessica was hiding. A moment of silence, then the doorknob slowly turned. The door was jammed and the man knew that Jessica was inside. He pushed the door with all his might and Jessica knew it was the end for one of them.

A man with an OC logo on his vest pushed through, falling on the ground from the impact while Jessica aimed at him. His gun dropped from his hands and he looked up at her. She was ready to fire but she hesitated. The man's heavy police helmet was the reason why she didn't. Jessica wasn't in the business of cop-killing unlike Francesco.

The man got up and took a step closer, removing his helmet and revealing his face. "Please?" pleaded Jessica. The man was Special Agent David Allen. "Run," whispered David as Jessica took a step closer to the window, still pointing her gun at him. "All is clear in here," shouted David turning around, shutting the door and heading back downstairs.

Jessica jumped out of the window, running on the wet roof. She then jumped onto the wet grass at the back side of the mansion. The garage door was already open and Sofia was sitting behind the wheel, with Luca in the back seat. Jessica ran to the car, getting inside. Before she closed the door, Sofia pulled off into the darkness of the night.

———

Jessica peaked behind her, watching the thick white fog

flying upwards from the Lombardi mansion, as the green lasers were still scanning the house. The OC Task Force recovered everything they needed to shut down Jessica's syndicate forever and indict her and anyone associated with her.

Sofia drove for close to an hour and everyone was dead tired and silent. The car wobbled every time as she kept hitting bumps on the dark road. Luca had fallen asleep in the back seat. The little guy didn't cry the whole time.

Jessica kept watching the night stars as the flashes of the street lamps passing by resembled shooting stars. She was grateful they survived and only by a miracle. One wrong move could have sent them all to the cemetery. Jessica had experienced yet another failure.

They have reached one of the secret safehouses of the Giulianis. The hideout was near the docks of the Hudson River. The perfect cover for escape because no one lived in the area except for the fishermen. Even the late Francesco never knew it existed. The safehouse was set up well before his birth during the first years of his father's business.

Sofia parked the car a block east of the hideout and carried Luca in her arms. Jessica walked alongside them holding her gun, inspecting the area. They kept walking until they reached an old building. Jessica couldn't help notice the graffiti, covering it from top to bottom. Outside of it was a statue of a redheaded woman with green eyes, holding the Statue of Liberty. It reminded Jessica of her holding New York in hers.

Sofia handed Luca to Jessica and went to open one of the doors. Jessica looked at the mailboxes in the reception area. Over ten residents were living there but she didn't recognize any of their names. They stood, waiting for the elevator to come down.

Once it reached, Sofia pulled aside its metal doors. The noise of the elevator's metal squeaked as they entered inside. Sofia pressed *number five*. The red button was rusted and the number was barely visible. The elevator went slowly and then stopped loudly. They exited to a large hallway which lead to a single door with a small number pad on the side.

Sofia pressed in the combination and a loud beep echoed the empty area. The metal bars on the door unlocked and Sofia pushed another keypad. Jessica assumed that this place was safer than Fort Knox. The door was comprised of four inches of steel, an electronic lock and sealing system which no one could enter even if a bomb exploded in front of it. Jessica was impressed.

The door opened slowly and they entered inside of the small unit. There weren't any windows and the room was lit up only by a few small bulbs in the ceiling.

Sofia walked further inside and opened a door on her right. She placed Luca in bed and closed the door behind her. Jessica waited for her in the living room, where she sat on the edge of a green couch.

"Sofia, I…"

"No, Jessica."

"I didn't ev-"

"I will not sit here and listen to your bullshit no longer. You are not thinking like someone who is capable of running an Italian family."

"Sofia, listen to me…"

"No, you'll listen to me, Jessica. Do we have to lose our lives for you to realize that it's over? Jacopo has taken over and warned you to leave. But no, your pride is more important, right?"

"No, Sofia. I'm sorry and you're right."

"I don't know why you take your son's life for play, Jessica. You act like you don't care if he lives or dies. I do and will not sit here to watch his precious life end for an impossible takeover that should have happened years ago."

"We talked about thi-"

"Yes, we did. A few days after my son and husband's funeral. It's over. They're dead! And whatever we do now will not bring them back."

"You know what, Sofia? I lost my husband, my grandmother, my father and everyone I loved that day, too. You're not the only one."

"Well, you didn't lose your precious son, Jessica! But you will if you keep acting like a ten-year-old seeking your father's approval."

Jessica's jaw dropped. She hadn't seen this side of Sofia before, not even on the day of the Bloodshed. Sofia's face showed that she was tired. Her voice was harsh as a killer in the moments before he takes a life. There was no remorse or sympathies. Only an old soul that was empty.

"Whether you like it or not Sofia, I will spend the remaining time I have left seeking what we came back here for. You might have forgotten, but I haven't."

"You are so naive, Jessica. The one who will suffer the burden of your loss is the boy in the other room. We can get medical treatment back in Italy and live a happy life once again. Oddio! At least for once, that merda Jacopo was right about you. That psychopath has outsmarted you."

"You're out of line, Sofia."

"My respect for your leadership left the moment you chose to put your life over your son's. We are Italians. Family always come first."

"I did not-"

"You did!" Sofia yelled, stressing the words coming out. Her eyes were like two pieces of charcoal. Jessica Sofia was like a bomb ready to explode. The anger inside her triggered her every body cell. A pause came as a needed break but the tension was unbearable as the two stared at each other.

"I want you to live, Jessica Lombardi. Strike but don't bring the fight into your home. Your father and my husband knew that. The moment they died, New York turned into turmoil and death reached our doorstep. Don't you ever forget that."

Jessica was ready to respond but Sofia's last words struck a note.

"Sofia, you're absolutely right. I will not bring death to our doorstep. But the moment this is all over, I will come back."

"Jessica. Don't say I didn't warn you."

"You have Mother Sofia."

"Now, go." Sofia couldn't keep fighting. Jessica turned around loading her gun and taking another before closing the door behind her.

## 33

## MY FINAL OFFER

Two days later, Sofia took Luca to school. She called in one of the Guilani bodyguards to accompany her. Even though everything in their lives was a mess right now, Sofia accepted the fact that the kid should attend school. Yet, a tiny whisper kept planting ideas that Luca would not be safe. Sofia couldn't let her life be dictated by Jessica's mistakes. Luca should attend school like a normal kid.

They were holding hands after being escorted out of the car. The cold morning breeze met their faces. The bodyguard was in front of them checking out the scene. Sofia adjusted Luca's jacket as his cheeks had developed a bright red color from the cold weather. They walked in silence even though they didn't speak much that morning. Luca still hadn't asked a single question about the new house or his mother. They kept walking and Luca tried not to step on the cracks of the sidewalk, a game he loved to play when he strolled with Jessica.

"Luca? Are you okay?"

"Yes, Grandma," said Luca nonchalantly, focusing on the cracks of the sidewalk.

"Are you excited about going back to school, sweetheart?"

"A little."

"You were more excited a few days ago."

"It made my mommy happy."

His words stabbed Sofia like a dagger in her heart. She smiled with sadness. *Damn you Jessica!*

"Is mommy gone?"

"No, Luca. Of course, not."

"Where is she?"

"She's working hard away from home."

"I miss her. She didn't make me breakfast this morning."

"I miss her too, Luca. She'll be back soon. Until then, I'll keep you company and make sure you have a good breakfast every morning."

"Okay." Luca said once again avoiding a big crack on the sidewalk as they reached outside his school.

"Here, we are. I'll be right here when you are done. Okay?"

"Okay, Grandma." Luca said as he crossed the street and entered the schoolyard. Sofia stood there looking at him. Luca would have trouble growing up without Jessica. She knew that and there wasn't much more she could offer him in comfort. The old woman already lost two children and wasn't willing to lose another.

Sofia walked away paying attention to her surroundings. She signaled the bodyguard to come closer as her eyes were still on Luca. "Stay here and make sure my grandson's safe."

"Yes, Donna Sofia."

She walked away and sat on a bench about a half block away from the school and opened her bag, taking out today's newspaper. *Still at large the culprits behind the massacre of Chinatown* was the front page headline. Sofia sighed and opened it.

As she turned the pages of the newspaper, she heard a set of footsteps fastly approaching her and a man had sat beside her. Sofia could see from the corner of her eye, the glare of the man's white suit. She gasped with fear, reaching for the gun inside her purse.

"Buongiorno, Sofia. Beautiful day today. Isn't it?" Jacopo said looking at the cloudy sky as if he was there for small talk.

"Leave us alone," said Sofia as she cocked her gun in her purse.

"Relax. If I wanted to hurt you, you'd already be dead, Sofia."

"What do you want, Jacopo?"

"To show my respect to Luca's wife. Is that okay?"

"Yeah right, Jacopo. Cut the bullshit."

"Sofia Guilani. I respected your husband. Luca was a

true leader. A firm man, but tough when times called for it."

"I know all that, Jacopo."

"When I was nothing but a Soldato, I wanted to be like Luca."

"Poor you."

"But I became wiser, Sofia."

"If that helps you sleep at night."

"Don't treat me like I'm some kind of animal like Michael Lombardi."

"Michael was a good man."

"And the reason why both your kids are dead."

"The reason my kids are dead is because of your fucking family, Jacopo."

"You know that's not true, Sofia. If Michael didn't make a deal against us, we would be but mere players at the table like everyone else. Isn't that so?"

"Shut it, or I will—Jacopo."

"Fierce, as always. I came to warn you Sofia. Just like I did with Jessica. I respect both of you. You deserve a chance."

"Warn me about what?"

"Things will get ugly for the Italian families who sided against me; for you and Jessica. Unless you leave town and never come back."

"Just like that? I leave and you forget about me?"

"I want New York, Sofia. I have nothing against you or Jessica. I don't hold grudges. Others do."

"Unfortunately, I don't trust you."

"I want to rule and I'm one small step away. Pack your stuff and leave. I want you out of New York first thing in the morning."

"I can't go back to the motherland. My grandson—"

"I don't care where you go but you must leave New York." Jacopo said getting up, fixing his suit. "This is the last time I'll be kind to you, Mama Sofia. Next time we meet, I'll be holding my gun." Jacopo smiled and walked away, staring at the cloudy sky, with the weak sunlight caressing his skin.

Sofia exhaled with relief as Jacopo walked away thinking *I won't make the same mistake as Jessica.*

---

Sofia didn't wait for a single second as she rushed back to the school, telling her bodyguard to get the car while she went inside to get Luca. Luca was confused, but didn't complain. Sofia returned to the hideout and reached above the vents in the ceiling. She pulled down bags of money, weapons and fake IDs. For close to twenty minutes, Sofia packed, glancing over the IDs and replacing the pictures. Half of them were already forged. She looked at the ones with Francesco's face and tried holding back her tears.

"Who is he?" Luca asked with great interest. "My son and a friend of your mother's." Sofia's voice cracked as she made a passport of Luca with a baby picture of him inside. Luca kept looking at an older man's picture in one of the passports. "And he, grandma?" said Luca pointing.

"That's your grandfather, my husband." Sofia felt the memories she had bottled inside for five years now were right there. She grabbed her passport, the bags and grabbed Luca's hand. "It's time to go on a trip."

"Will Mommy be coming?"

"Yes, I believe so. I'll leave her a note, so she can meet us."

Sofia left a note in one of the empty bags and threw it on the couch. She took a moment to check everything around her, making sure she had everything she needed. A few seconds later, she exited with Luca and locked the hideout. It was time to get out of New York for good.

## 34

## WHAT THE HECK?

Almost two months have now passed, and the spring was giving its place to the warm winds of the early summer. Jessica had her eyes half-open. The apartment was covered with newspapers lying everywhere. The television was on, broadcasting the news, with reporters and show hosts still talking about the Chinatown incident.

It's been rough for Jessica. She kept a low-profile in New York City, always dying her hair, changing her appearance and renting apartments no longer than a week at a time. This was the tenth one. Jessica cut her hair low and even changed eye colors by getting contacts. Sofia and Luca were nowhere to be found. The hideout was vacant as it was before the only night she went there. There was a letter was left behind reading: *We will be where it all started.* Sofia had written it in handwriting.

Apart from the letter, there were a few weapons left behind and some bags of money.

Jessica had missed the old Guilani woman who was her biggest supporter and more than anyone, her son, Luca Guilani. She turned over still feeling that burning sensation inside her chest. Her lungs begged for a cigarette but desperately needed fresh air. Jessica felt she was getting weaker but she kept resisting the thoughts of death. It wasn't over yet. Everything felt like it was except her will. She had one goal left - to kill Jacopo. Jessica sat up in her bed and lit up a cigarette, turning up the volume on the television:

*The parties responsible behind the Chinatown Incident are still at large. NYPD and the respective law enforcement agencies have abstained from making any official statements, however there are unnamed sources that have mention a few organizations that could have masterminded the massacre. What is known is that a new plague of organized crime have rotted our city from within.*

*OC Task Force, Special Agent David Allen has never released an official statement on whether the Chinatown Incident was a result of the Italian Mafia rivals at war with one another or the work of other rival gangs including the Triads.*

*In other news, Jacopo Saltinotti of New York City's 7th District has become the top candidate for New York's upcoming mayoral race in recent polls.*

The reporter stopped as a footage clip came on screen of Jacopo talking in Central Park. Jessica muted the TV. She was sick of hearing his name and grabbed yesterday's newspaper, searching for something interesting. Something she didn't already knew. *"Jacopo for Mayor"* ad columns were posted throughout. "If these New Yorkers fall for giving the mob total control over the city, let it be. If they elect Jacopo to office, this city would crumble in 24 hours," she thought to herself.

Jessica reached an article on page 8 which she didn't expect to find:

### Suspected Philanthropist Found Dead

*Julius Fonda, the well-known investor and philanthropist was found murdered in his apartment yesterday. He died from a bullet wound to the head. The legendary benefactor of New York was found dead on arrival. Mob experts believe that this was a mob hit but nothing is confirmed as yet.*

*Special Agent David Allen has released the following statement: "We don't know who would want to hurt such an honest man. Our job is to shed light on the truth once evidence is uncovered."*

*There aren't no more official statements from New York's law enforcement agencies on the matter of Julius' death at this time. There were no signs of forced entry in Mr. Fonda's apartment.*

Jessica put paper down, dawning on the outcome.

Julius was the last of the capofamiglia in New York. The only one who was a threat to Jacopo from the men of old. Jessica took out a pair of scissors and cut out the article. She held it up saying *"Pace al'anima sua!"*

The article reminding her of her failures, stubbornness and pride and what it has done to her associates. She opened the paper again; Page 10 caught her attention with the headline reading:

### Money Extortion by New York's Head Priest

*The head priest of Saint Peter's Church of Manhattan, Paolo Episcopo, the descendant of the well-known family of priests has been taken to court after the IRS, with the help of FBI and ATF made a thorough investigation into his churches' assets for months.*

*After weeks of tracing through anonymous bank accounts and shell companies, Paolo Episcopo has been found laundering money for an unknown investor through the churches of Manhattan and all the assets owned by the church have confiscated.*

*Now sentenced, defendant Paolo Episcopo will spend the rest of his natural life in prison. He's being held at the Lincoln Correctional Facility of New York awaiting transfer to a high-level maximum security prison upstate. His name has been tied to many allegations of involvement in organized crime activities, with many suspecting that he was involved directly in the Chinatown Incident, but these allegations are substantial.*

*Paolo Episcopo has abstained from making any official statements to the press. Special Agent David Allen, the head of OC Task Force has released the following statement. "We believe Paolo Episcopo was laundering money for many of the criminal networks besides the Italian. Ultimately, we are happy that justice prevailed and Paolo Episcopo has gotten what he deserved.*

Suddenly, a new flash alert popped on the screen reading:

### *Mafia Church Boss murdered in Prison*

*This just in… Paolo Episcopo, the convicted money launderer was assassinated last evening at the Lincoln Correctional Facility where he was being held, waiting to serve a life sentence. Three stabs wounds to the chest from an improvised shiv made from duct tape and razors. The man behind Episcopo's assassination was being transferred to the same super max facility upstate and was hours away from being transported along with Mr. Episcopo and others.*

"*Pace al'anima sua!*" said Jessica as she sat motionless. A few minutes later, she opened the paper and when she got to page 16, the headline read:

### *Jewish Drug Lord of New York found slain*

*Alexander Aaron Lavie, the notorious drug lord of New York City was hospitalized, three nights ago, at the Queens Hospital facility after he was a victim of a hit and run. Mister Lavie was placed in a medically-induced coma after suffering massive head trauma. After a series of emergency surgeries in a desperate attempt to save Mr. Lavie's life, the hospital was unsuccessful in reviving him after his heart suddenly stopped beating.*

*The people of New York upon hearing the death of Mr. Lavie cheered in Manhattan Square. Many honking their horns at the news.*

*The police are still investigating the hit-and-run incident but so far, there have been no leads. There are no official statements given by law enforcement at this time.*

Sadness filled Jessica's heart. The Saltinottis murdered poor Julius and Paolo. How about Andrea? She hoped Andrea wouldn't be found at the bottom of New York Harbor. Jessica held back her tears, slowly closing the paper.

———

Now that the heads of the families were either dead or missing, she had nothing to lose. Sofia and Luca are on their way to Canada. There was nothing stopping Jessica now from finishing it all. She would be dead sooner or later.

Jessica's attention turned up the volume on the television once again and waited patiently until the top of the hour when the first headline read on the screen:

*Mayoral Candidate, Jacopo Saltinotti will be giving a speech in 90 minutes outside the 7th Precinct in support of the martyrs of the Chinatown Incident.*

Jessica laughed, "In support of who? This *Figlio di Puttana* has some fucking nerve." She made peace with her deteriorating health but would never make peace for the deaths of her family members. If there was to be one last stand, it would be for them.

Jessica got up, dressing in a black dress, white scarf and black sunglasses. She looked at herself in the mirror. White as snow, her skin was pale. The dark bags under her eyes made her look like she was a drug addict. Jessica almost looked older than Sofia even though she was almost forty-five years younger. Her lips were chapped and her hair was a mess. It wouldn't matter in a few hours from now.

She grabbed her gun and put it inside her purse. It was time to attend Jacopo's public speech.

## 35

## REVENGE

Cameras were set in front of the 7th precinct around a wooden podium, placed for Jacopo Saltinotti.

A huge crowd was gathered with reporters waiting to get an exclusive of Jacopo, the soon-to-be politician whose numbers were rising slowly in the city's polls. The chatter of the people there filled the air as everyone waited in suspense.

Jessica walked through the crowd, pushing her way close to the podium. Her eyes were set on the steps of the precinct and kept visualizing the moment that Jacopo would come out. She wanted a clear view of him, ignoring those who were cursing as she pushed through the crowd. She avoided the little wooden tables giving away free pins and t-shirts writing *'Say NO to organized crime'*. That was Jacopo's campaign slogan. He was selling himself as a philanthropist who wanted to end crime in the city of New York. *Oh! How convenient?*

Eventually, she reached the closest she could. There was a perimeter around the area guarded by agents carrying semi-automatic weapons, wearing bulletproof vests. Jessica glanced up at the roofs across the street. FBI snipers were positioned on every rooftop. Jacopo clearly had the support of the law enforcement on his side.

The crowd grew restless as the time passed until finally the doors of the precinct opened and Jacopo walked down the steps, surrounded by agents led by the head of the OC Task Force, David Allen and to Jessica's surprise, her husband, Alberto Caruso standing in the back of Jacopo.

Jacopo looked at the crowd in awe and waved. He was savoring every minute he could. He closed his eyes and took a deep breath, letting the moment soak in as the light summer breeze passed through his slick black hair. A barrage of camera flashes made him look like a rock star at a Fourth of July concert. The reporters shouted, trying to get Jacopo's attention, but he kept staring straight ahead.

Jacopo raised his hand for everyone to be silent. "Citizens of New York. Thank you all for coming here today to show your supports to the families of the victims of an incident that has stained New York's history once again. We hope to leave these heartbroken memories behind from now on. We hope for a better future…" Jacopo sounded like a real politician moving his hands up and down and choosing his words carefully. Jacopo kept talking and Jessica ignored him.

For a moment, everything around her turned silent. Jessica felt like she was treading the bottom of the sea. She could see Jacopo's lips moving, but only humming reached her ears. She closed her eyes and when she opened them, she saw Alberto glancing over at her. He was shocked. Jessica place her hand inside her purse.

Alberto knew why Jessica was there. "Please, Jessica. Don't," whispered Alberto, only moving his lips but Jessica turned to Jacopo. She felt nothing, pulling out her gun and pointed it at Jacopo. The soft buzzing that reached her ears was disrupted as the FBI agents screamed, "That lady's got a gun. Get down." The crowd ran like ants in the desert. Jessica pulled the trigger and Jacopo ducked with the bullet missing him.

The crowd was gone, leaving Jessica standing alone in the middle. Alberto's eyes teared up and David watched with an expression of surprise and grieve. In a glimpse of seconds, Jessica was tackled to the ground, feeling a strong thrust from one of the agents. Her gun was knocked out of her hand, falling a few feet away.

Jessica landed hard on the ground, hitting her head. Tears were coming down her eyes as the agents restrained her as they put her in handcuffs. "No!" Jessica screamed. "No. This isn't right!" She kept screaming as an agent pulled her up off the ground, dragging her towards to an unmarked police car. "No! You don't understand. Jacopo's the one who did the Chinatown

Incident. No!" Jessica kept screaming at the top of her lungs, coughing up blood. She couldn't scream any longer as her lungs had given up.

The agent pushed her inside the car and locked the door. Jessica stared straight ahead in the unmarked car. She wanted to scream, but she felt weak and exhausted.

"What should we do with her?" asked an agent to David Allen who rushed towards the car.

"We can't keep her here. Take her downtown. Hurry!" said David, turning his back to the car as the agent sat behind the wheel. Jessica could only hear chattering without words. One agent tried speaking to her but she couldn't hear anything. Her life was ruined.

Jessica leaned back and closed her eyes as the unmarked car left the scene with two others flashing lights and sirens. She closed her eyes, and she felt a warm feeling washing over her body. It was over and time to make peace. Jessica kept her eyes closed and never opened them again.

———

Jessica took her last breath long before the police car reached the downtown precinct. The officers thought she was sleeping but when they discovered she was unresponsive, it was already too late. Jessica left the world unable to seek revenge and never got the chance to say goodbye.

The incident of Jessica Lombardi dying in the back of a police car reached the papers faster than Jacopo's reaction speech about the incident. For the next month, it was the only thing that kept playing on television, daily newspapers and tabloids.

*Jessica Lombardi, the daughter of the late Italian Godfather, Michael Lombardi and bride of the late infamous mafia underboss, Francesco Giuliani was found dead in the back of a police car after a failed attempted murder of incumbent mayor-in-running candidate, Jacopo Saltinotti. The ruthless woman who was one of the co-conspirators behind the tragic Bloodshed event came back to New York City to destroy its peace.*

The media crucified her as more and more as wild rumors surfaced. As a result of her death, the OC Task Force's investigation on organized crime gained national fame and notoriety. Jessica Lombardi was demonized, known as the woman who made New York bleed in less time than the Gotti family. Some citizens admired her for the raw determination she possessed while others set out to smear her name.

Coincidently, the New York press idolized Jacopo as a true survivor after the assassination attempt. This only strengthened his base of supporters. Through a series of backdoor payments and blackmailing, Jacopo had articles published in the city's papers that made him look like a hero. Most stated were smear campaigns of the Lombardis, Baldinottis and Guilanis.

Ten days later, Jacopo had won the mayoral elections, thus becoming New York City's new mayor.

## 36

## TYING UP LOOSE ENDS

Jacopo was sitting behind the desk inside his mahogany office at City Hall. It has been a few days since his first term began and he was starstruck. Jacopo managed to outsmart all of his enemies. Now revered in the public's eye, Jacopo's hidden agenda was just beginning.

Using his position's power, Jacopo hunted down anyone who conflicted with his business. In the promise of cleaning up the city, he gave New York's citizens want they wanted while his organized crime activities would go unnoticed. Jacopo achieved what Jessica was striving for.

Jacopo looked outside the old window, sipping a glass of wine, letting its beautiful scent tease his nostrils. It was his way of smelling his successes. The door knocked and David Allen entered.

"Mr. Mayor," said David disgusted, not believing he was calling the crime lord of New York, *'mayor.'*

"Agent Allen, please have a seat."

"You asked to see me, sir?"

"Yes, I did. May I offer you a glass of wine?"

"No, thank you. I don't drink while I'm on duty, sir."

*"Agent of the Year!"* mocked Jacopo taking another sip, then putting the glass down.

"My job here is done, sir. I'm handing in my resignation effective tomorrow. The HQ in DC needs me more than here."

"I know. That's why I called to see you, Agent Allen."

"Is there anything else?"

"Yes, there is. I'm tying up loose ends. You see, my position is still volatile, even more now that I'm the mayor of New York City. I don't want my past relationships to haunt me. I hope you understand, Agent."

"I do, sir but I don't understand your point."

"You are part of those past relationships. I know you are a loose cannon, David."

"What are you saying?"

"I'm saying that I can't let you run away with all the things you know about me."

"I did what you asked of me. What else do you want?"

"You are thereby terminated."

"You can't just fire me. I'm in charge of the OC investigation. Would you like another investigation that would implicate you and—," said David before he was interrupted.

"I assure that all the evidence I have on you, David Allen can be made public."

"False evidence!"

"Can you prove that?"

"I'll just resign. You'll never see me again. Let me resign in the next 24 hours and you won't hear from me ever again. "

"I'm afraid that's a little too late, David. FBI agents are already at the door to escort you out."

"What if I were to kill you right here, right now?"

"You know you won't do that, David. You know how many innocent lives would suffer if you did that."

"You're a sick fuck, Jacopo."

"That's what I've heard all of my life. I would consider myself a nice person."

David stood up, grabbing his service weapon and pointed it at Jacopo but right before he could pull the trigger, the door slammed open and four agents swarmed the room. The silent conversation gave precedence to a series of shouts. "Drop it, Allen or I'll shoot!" an agent shouted, pointing his gun to the back of David's head. "You all don't get it. Jacopo is the criminal behind New York's organized crime," said David as he put down his weapon and placed his hands behind his head.

"David Allen, you are thereby being charged with murder, kidnapping, conspiracy and…" An agent said arresting David and placing handcuffs on him.

"Jacopo's behind all the crime in the city," shouted David.

"You have the right to remain silent. Everything you say can and will be used against you in the court of law. Do you understand, David Allen?"

"No, you don't get it. He's the real criminal." David struggled as an agent pulled David down to the ground.

"Sorry for this, Mr. Mayor," said one of the agents.

Jacopo looked surprised, "Thank you, officers. I'm glad you were here in time. I could have died."

"We are sorry again," an agent said taking David away. The moment the door closed, Jacopo stood up smiling and staring at the street with his hands crossed behind his back. It was officially over. All loose ends had been taken care of. Jacopo Saltinotti was the new Godfather of New York. Everything and everyone was under his control and the law was on his side.

The court date for David Allen took place in less than a month which was highly unusual. He faced a life sentence with the possibility of no parole. David Allen was found guilty of all the charges as the evidence against him was compelling. Jacopo found witnesses willing to testify against David and the case was wrapped up in the twinkling of an eye. He was sentenced to spend the rest of his days on Earth in a 6 x 8 jail cell.

David woke up screaming, gasping for air and his body was sweating bullets. Rivers of sweat had flooded his white sheets. He looked around at the white walls of his cell and cried like a child who was punished for stealing from his mother's cookie jar. Then, David went back to sleep, dreaming he was a free man.

———

It's been a week since his incarceration and the same dream visited David every night. He saw himself as a free man back at the FBI, awarded with the FBI Shield of Bravery for his service in ridding New York City of organized crime. David cried he woke up at night because of his harsh reality - *life in prison without parole.*

Tears came down his cheeks as David reflected on having the ideal American life. A great job he loved so much was no longer. He was so close to being honored, deeming himself better than Agent Miller. David was blinded in opposite to the career of Agent Thomas Miller.

He was similar to Jessica - ambitious but life had other plans. His career in law enforcement was like Icarus flying too close to the sun. His wings had melted and then fell helplessly into the Earth's atmosphere.

David struggled to see the bright side and rightfully so. He kept thinking about proving Jacopo was a criminal. When he had phone calls, he tried finding media that wanted to hear his side of the story. No one wanted to take the chance because Jacopo had everyone in his pocket.

The jail's inmates were already against David, threatening him and making his life a living hell. None of them knew he worked for the FBI. The moment they did, he would end up dead. It was his stand-offish attitude that made friends inside difficult. The man who used to apprehend these thugs was now the criminal. He couldn't even share a plate of food with them. *"Lights out! Inmates,"* yelled the guards. It was another day of David's new life.

The next morning, the buzzing sound of his cell door alarmed and it had opened. A prison guard stood outside his cell, watching him closely. "6104, you have a visitor," said the guard smiling.

"Visitor, early this morning?" David asked worried, unable to shake off the feeling of sleep.

An inmate suddenly came to the cell's door, holding a shank. "Jacopo Saltinotti says hello." He rushed in, stabbing David continuously to the gut. The inmate threw him down to the floor and kicked him in the face. He threw the shank in David's toilet and exited quickly.

"Cell Block 6104 close!" shouted the guard and the door was closed.

David was bleeding to death on the floor. Even in prison, Jacopo had manpower. "God forgive me for my sins," said David holding his stomach, trying to stop the blood which was splashing out like a small fountain.

His life, career and memories were all fading into darkness. David then realized he was no better than Thomas Miller. Miller gave up his life taking down mobsters even if his way was unconventional. David Allen would die here, known for working for organized crime.

Within three minutes, Special Agent David Allen was dead.

The FBI did not bother looking further into the case

of David Allen extensively as they portrayed him - *The Traitor who betrayed the citizens of New York.* His past legacy locking up criminals was quickly forgotten as David became the most hated man in New York replacing Jessica Lombardi in the tabloids.

## 37

## PRISON

Sofia drove silently through the off-and-on storms that were predicted for the day. Luca was sound asleep in the backseat. They have been traveling for four hours to upstate New York. She had been driving through forests, lakesides and saw everything that nature had to offer. The radio was on, but she didn't pay much attention to it. Sofia had heard all she needed to hear. Jacopo was now mayor of New York City and Jessica was dead along with the other Italian family members. The news reporters kept talking on the same subject, hour by hour. Non-stop analysis and debates with organized crime experts flooding the airwaves. Everyone had their own point of view.

Sofia kept going until she reached the outside of a prison. She got out and opened the backdoor. "Luca sweetheart, wake up." She said softly as Luca opened his eyes. "Are we there, Grandma?"

"Yes, we are. Come on, honey." She helped Luca out of the car seat and they began walking in the direction of the large correctional facility, whose towering walls were blocking the sunlight.

The guard sitting inside the booth cautiously looked at Sofia. "Identification, Ma'am." Sofia slid her ID through the small slot under the window.

"Sign here," said the guard pushing a piece of paper towards her. Sofia, signed and handed it back.

"Is this young lad your son, Ms. Johnson?"

"Yes, it is."

"Visiting hours are over in one hour," said the guard pressing a button on a panel in front of him.

A loud buzzing sounded, as the iron door slid open, revealing the interior of the prison. Sofia grabbed Luca by the hand and walked forward. "Why did you lie about your name, Grandma?" asked Luca. "Sometimes, it's better that way. You'll see," answered Sofia without having a better excuse. *How could she tell this child they were being hunted and she could end up in jail or dead?*

"But why so, Grandma?"

"Because Luca." Her serious tone made Luca look down at the ground. Sofia felt bad she couldn't explain further. Luca was too small.

The two walked through the prison yard. Men in orange uniforms were standing behind big iron gates, looking at the two. "Where are you going, grandma?" An inmate shouted from the back, followed by the laughs of his buddies. Sofia ignored them and pulled Luca closer to her. She kept walking until the guards opened another gate leading to the inside the prison.

Sofia entered inside with Luca. Their footsteps mirrored the white marble floor as they proceeded further inside. Yelling and shouting deafened their ears as a group of inmates were fighting and guards were there breaking it up. They headed to the infirmary where a nurse was sitting outside, smoking. "I'm sorry, Miss. Can I leave my son here for a moment? I don't want to take him inside," asked Sofia kindly.

The nurse didn't mind and Luca sat beside her. "Luca, I'll be back in a few minutes. Okay? Be nice to the kind lady here, okay?" Sofia patted Luca on the head. "Okay," said Luca taking out one of his favorite books which he would read for the millionth time.

----

Sofia walked from gate to gate. The buzzing sound echoed as she made her way to the sitting area. The place was crowded with women, children and relatives of the inmates. There were six guards were patrolling up and down the room. "Hands above the table," shouted the guards from time to time. Sofia grew impatient waiting.

The buzzing sound echoed again. "Inmate 18459, your visitor's here," shouted a guard pointing at Sofia as she stood up.

Jessica's brother, Giovanni walked through the iron

gate and headed towards her. "Sofia!" he called out coming closer to embrace her. *"No hugs allowed, inmate!"* Giovanni stopped to sit across Sofia with his hands above the table.

"Sofia, you look great." Giovanni uttered with a genuine sentiment. He was desperate to see such a noble face.

"How are you?"

"I've been better but I'm glad you are doing okay. I should have come sooner."

"It's okay."

"How are things inside?"

"It was hard at first. But now, I made my peace with it. Our families' names still have respect inside."

"It's good to hear that."

"Where's my sister? And Luca?"

"I left Luca with the nurse at the infirmary."

"Why, is he hurt?"

"No, he's okay. I just didn't want to bring him inside here to see this madness at such a young age."

"And Jessica?"

"I'm sorry but I have some bad news, Giovanni."

"Sofia!"

"Jessica…" Sofia paused trying to explain, but her eyes said it. Giovanni's smile vanished and his eyes teared.

"Please tell me it's not so, Sofia."

"I'm afraid it is not, Giovanni."

"Who was behind it?"

"No one."

"Then what the hell happened?"

"She died of lung cancer."

"Jessica died of what? You must be kidding."

"I'm afraid I am not. But even if she didn't, she would have spent the rest of her days in prison."

"But how?"

"We lost to Jacopo. All of the family heads are dead and we are now on the run."

"That fucking stronzo! I will kill that bastardo!"

Giovanni and Sofia sat in silence and then their conversation resumed.

"When was Jessica's funeral?"

"A week ago."

"Did anyone attend?"

"No one."

"How come?"

"Everyone is dead, Giovanni. The Italian family heads have been killed off or are missing. We have no more protection."

"Because of Jacopo?"

"Yes. He was elected mayor of New York over two weeks ago and now he's in charge of everything."

Giovanni clutched his fists. "That *brutto figlio di puttana*? How did he defeat our families?"

"Her husband, Alberto was working for him all along."

"You're joking, right?"

"I'm afraid not. This and the fact that Jessica made many mistakes."

"I was afraid something like this would end up happening. What made you came here today?"

"I came here to warn you, Giovanni."

"About what?"

"Jacopo's tying up loose ends. Not only in his own circle but everywhere. He's taking out anyone he deems as a threat. Be careful, my son."

"I have nothing to be afraid of. I'm well connected in here."

"Jacopo's crazy, Giovanni."

Giovanni and Sofia sat in silence momentarily and then resumed their conversation.

"Where are you going now?"

"We're headed to Canada. We'll hide there for some time. After that, I do not know."

"How's Luca?"

"He knows nothing. I'd like to keep it that way, at least for now."

"He deserves to know."

"And he will. Not now. He's already suffered enough. Jacopo tried to kill us but we escaped."

Giovanni sobbed and shook his head.

"Visiting time is over. Inmates, line up!" a guard yelled and Giovanni stood up.

"It was a pleasure seeing you, Sofia. I wish we had more time. Be safe and take care of my nephew."

"I will, my son. I'll come back, Giovanni. Whatever you need, call this number." Sofia wrote it down.

"Va bene! Arrivederci!" said Giovanni as the inmates were lining up to be escorted back to their cells.

Sofia left the visiting area and took Luca back to the car. They headed up the long road to Canada where they would spend time until the dust settled.

———

Giovanni walked in a straight row with the other inmates back to their cells. "Hands against the wall. Search time!" shouted a guard and all the inmates turned around, placing their hands on the wall, spreading their legs. Giovanni saw an inmate, looking at him weirdly.

"What are you looking at, you fucking faggot?"

"A dead man. Lombardi fucking scum," shouted the inmate. Before Giovanni could react, the inmate repeatedly thrusted his shiv in Giovanni's stomach. Seconds later, his throat was slit.

The guards went to apprehend the inmate but it was too late. The inmate was already kneeling on the ground with his hands behind his head, yelling "Greetings from Jacopo, you fucking *figlio di Puttana*." A guard kicked the inmate in the face, knocking him unconscious.

"Nurse! An inmate is dying!" shouted the guards on their radios. Giovanni Lombardi was drowning in his own pool of blood, coughing it up like a volcano. The thought of meeting Jessica and his family in the afterlife made him smile momentarily. He saw them laughing and talking at the family table as darkness overcame him. A warm sensation disseminated over him as his blood soaked most of his orange uniform. He closed his eyes and in a matter of seconds, his soul departed the world. Jacopo Saltinotti made sure to tie up loose ends or did he?

www.ingramcontent.com/pod-product-compliance
Lightning Source LLC
Chambersburg PA
CBHW060927190726
48286CB00002B/666